Acclaim for *Tobacco Republic*

"Readers will be enthralled by R. A. Moss's exceptional storytelling, making *Tobacco Republic* both a provocative and unforgettable read. I highly recommend this book."
—Alan Collenette, *Historical Novel Society*

"A crackling spy thriller set like a jewel in a wild but timely counterhistory."
—Charlie Haas, author of *The Current Fantasy* and *The Enthusiast*

"Lovers of spy novels know that fast-paced treachery, betrayal, and gamesmanship are almost always fun. In this novel, they are thought-provoking, too."
—Rebecca Coffey, author of *Hysterical: Anna Freud's Story*

"High recommendation to readers and book clubs"
—D. Donovan, Senior Reviewer, *Midwest Book Reviews*

"This fascinating novel will appeal to anyone interested in American history.'"
—John Kachuba, author of *Shapeshifters: A History*

"A perfect book for our dangerously fractured times."
—Jennifer Silva Redmond, author of *Honeymoon at Sea: How I Found Myself Living on a Small Boat*

"A wonderfully inventive and graceful novel."
—John Thorndike, author of *The World Against Her Skin* and *The Passionate Sister*

Beck and Branch Publishers
New York, NY | beckandbranch.com
ISBN: 979-8-9926682-0-9

Public Domain Illustration Sources:
Library of Congress, Creative Commons, Pexels.com

AN ALTERNATIVE HISTORY

TOBACCO REPUBLIC

WHAT IF THE THIRTEEN COLONIES NEVER UNITED?

R.A. MOSS

BECK & BRANCH PUBLISHERS

For those who look far enough ahead

to see the past

QUEBEC ★

Massa-
chusetts
BOSTON ★

New York
ALBANY ★

People's
Republic of
Pennsylvania
PHILADELPHIA ★

New Francia

Virginia
RICHMOND ★

THE SEVEN
NATIONS
OF THE
**BRITANNIC
REGION**

North
Carolina ★ RALEIGH

South
Carolina
CHARLESTON ★

Georgia
SAVANNAH ★

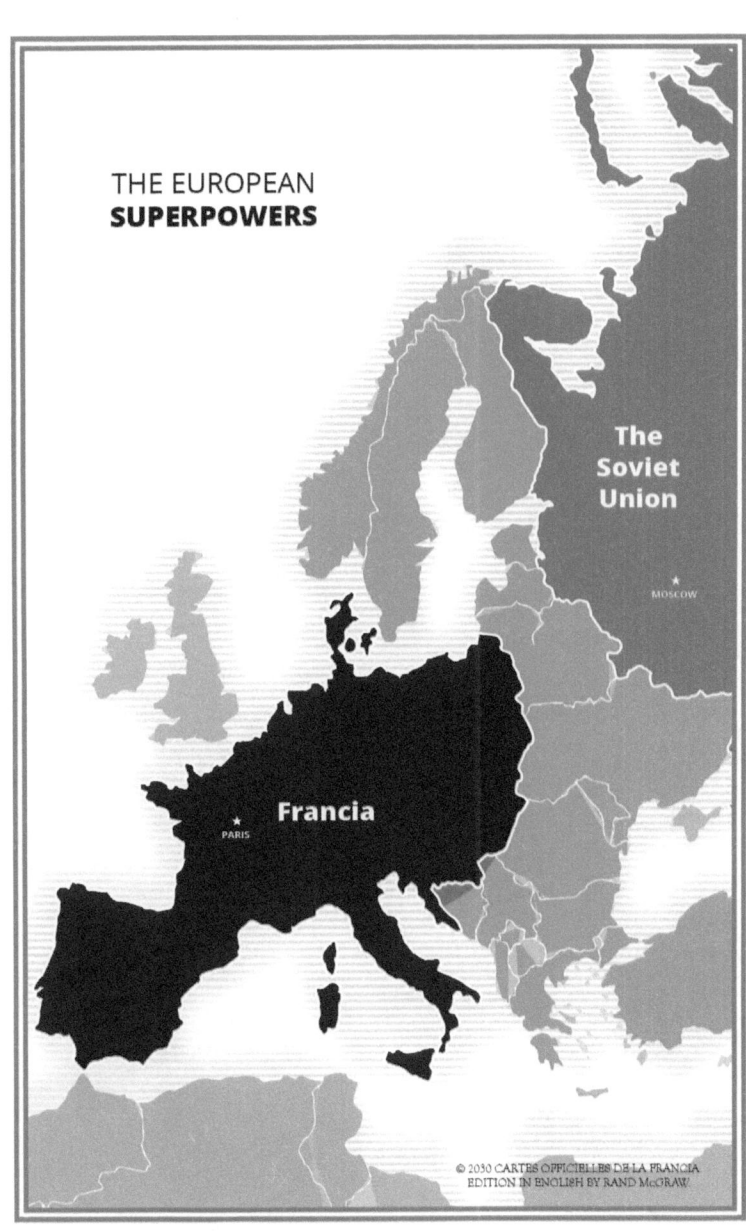

1776

PHILADELPHIA, PENNSYLVANIA

The familiar scent of sweat, tobacco and horse dung assailed Thomas Jefferson as he entered the assembly room at the Pennsylvania State House. Over fifty members of the Second Continental Congress were settling into curved-back chairs around thirteen tables covered in green wool. The president of the congress had yet to gavel the session into order and the drone of the delegates' voices brought a hornet swarm to mind for Jefferson.

To Jefferson's chagrin, few of the representatives turned to acknowledge his entrance.

As a relentless advocate for unifying the colonies, Jefferson had become a pariah – even within the ranks of his fellow delegates from Virginia. George Washington, a popular member of his legation, had taken particular relish in calling Jefferson's writing "dainty flowers scattered in the wind."

Four days ago, the assembled delegates had passed the Lee Resolution, drafted by another Virginian, that asserted the thirteen colonies were now sovereign states and no longer part of England. The stage seemed set for Jefferson to fulfill his long-held hope: to unite the colonies into a single nation. He had even privately commissioned a flag for the new republic.

His elation was short-lived.

Yesterday, Jefferson's Declaration of Independence had been voted down, primarily for the use of four words he refused to change: the United States of America

Undaunted, Jefferson planned to resurrect his cause today. After more than a year in the Continental Congress, he had learned that loyalties could be fleeting. With the right leverage, a delegate's stance on an issue could be encouraged to change. And Jefferson believed there was one man with the power to influence others who might still be persuaded.

Walking to the Massachusetts table, the Virginian approached Samuel Adams. "May I have a word, sir?" he asked demurely.

Adams stood, removed the pipe from his lips and studied Jefferson for a moment. "Speak your piece," he finally said.

"Mister Adams, under what terms would you consider ratifying my Declaration?"

"Why would Massachusetts ratify your document, Jefferson? If we join these so-called United States you propose, a state like Virginia with a larger population can dictate policies favorable to your economy, not ours. Our people farm, they fish, they ply trades. They don't own plantations that need large numbers of slaves to be profitable. All your fancy words on liberty don't amount to a pail of hog slop if Massachusetts is not equal to Virginia in deciding our best interests.

"In a republic, every state would have delegates equal to their population. That's certainly fair, is it not?"

Adams sneered. "And in the meantime, you'll count the negroes in Virginia as part of your population to increase the number of your delegates."

"I'm sure we can reach a compromise to take that property into account."

"Would you agree to a tax on this *property* you speak of?"

Jefferson shook his head. "Unfortunately, we cannot. A tax on slaves would bankrupt the plantations. Our income on the export of tobacco barely covers our expenses."

"Is that so?" Adams said, arching an eyebrow. "And what of the native tribes in our colonies? They outnumber us in many places. Will they count toward your representation?"

"Tribal lands do not conform to the borders of our colonies. To include them would—"

A sudden clamor interrupted their conversation. All eyes turned toward the door.

Walking slowly with a cane, Benjamin Franklin entered the chamber. A swell of bodies moved toward Franklin, offering greetings and handshakes.

"There's the man you should persuade," Adams said to the Virginian.

Unknown to Adams, Franklin had already privately rejected his idea. "I favor unity among our colonies in resistance to the king's tyranny, Jefferson. But you take matters too far," the old man had said. "We already have too many Germans in Pennsylvania. Your scheme of a single nation would open our borders and attract larger herds of Palatine boors."

Instead, Jefferson turned to Adams. "I believe your support carries more weight."

The flattery drew a mild smile from Adams. But his face grew stern again. "The idea of unification is dead, Jefferson. Your energies are better spent helping us resolve more pressing matters. We've yet to decide how we'll tax goods across our borders. And we still have a war to fight against the lobsterbacks."

"But if we unify, our chances of regulating taxes and defeating the British will —"

Adams raised his palm, cutting him off. "Jefferson, the purpose of this congress is to form an alliance that will help our colonies defeat a common enemy. Very few men in this room are ready to sacrifice their sovereignty for your fanciful cause."

Stymied, Jefferson decided the time had come to play his strongest card. Through discreet inquiries, the Virginian had learned that Adams' main source of income was producing malt for beer fermentation – despite being a Puritan teetotaler.

"Mister Adams," Jefferson said, tenting his fingers, "it's possible I can persuade the Virginia delegation to support a tax rate favorable for producers of malt – if you can find your way clear to support unification."

Adams glared at the Virginian, his eyes narrowing. "What do you take me for, sir? Do you think my support can be bought?" he said, seething. "Walk away, Mister Jefferson. Walk away before I forget my vows against violence."

Lowering his eyes, Jefferson left the chamber. No one noticed his departure.

Alone on the street, he stared down at the dung-smeared cobblestones. Persuading Adams had been his last hope. He had to face the truth.

His dream of a United States of America was gone.

~=~

| Day One |
THE PRESENT

PARIS, FRANCIA

My walk to work that morning would have looked like any other.

At least, that's what I hoped as I left my apartment. My life depended on it.

I passed the tourists along Avenue Foch ambling toward the Arc de Triomphe. They were the usual bunch, rocking active sportswear, taking selfies, counting the steps on their fitraks, and puffing on vapes that fogged the air with fruit-infused tobacco.

Adjusting the scarf over my hair, I furtively scanned the sightseers, looking for SS agents. The crowd was a prime spot to start shadowing a mark.

I was safe for the moment. The *Services de Sécurité* spies were easy to spot. Their haughty stares betrayed them.

Everyone connected with the government of Francia – including their covert operatives – carried themselves with an air that said, *we rule the world*. They just couldn't help themselves, the arrogant pricks.

I'll say this much for the toads, though. They had more respect for career women like me in Francia than in my own hidebound country. But that didn't make me hate the toads any less – or feel any safer.

As a military liaison at Virginia's embassy in Paris, I had good reason to worry about SS surveillance. With a war brewing between Virginia and Pennsylvania, Francia was keeping a close eye on the diplomats from both nations – despite being an ally of Virginia. The toads did not trust Britannics, the ethnic label for people from the English-speaking nations of North America.

Their suspicions weren't wrong. That's why picking up an SS tail would have put my life at risk.

I was part of a clandestine operation in the heart of Paris. If all went according to plan, in nine days, the Arc de Triomphe would be ground zero for a massive detonation. That attack would launch Germany's war of independence from Francia – and strike a blow against the toads' oppression in Virginia as well.

| Day Two |

CHARLOTTESVILLE, VIRGINIA

What Brody Linn had learned from his mole inside the Virginia Security Agency was hazy: Francia had secretly deployed a new ordnance unit to the National Guard armory in Charlottesville. Very unusual. Very hush-hush. His mole's name was Lily and pillow talk was always sketchy.

Sex with the enemy was part of Brody's job as a spy for the People's Republic of Pennsylvania. The reason was not surprising. The surest way to crack another nation's security was not through a tech hack. Human vices were the most reliable passkey: greed, vanity and, of course, sex. But it still made Brody uneasy.

As a kid, his mother had been a sex worker. Now he was using sex as part of his own work. The irony was a painful reminder of the burden his mother had endured to provide for him while she was alive.

Despite his qualms, when Brody passed on Lily's intel to his boss in Philly, Brody quickly found himself heading to Charlottesville.

"You get to bell the cat, son," his boss had said.

The assignment was not surprising. Brody had earned a reputation as his section's go-to guy for risky ops. No complaints on his part, though. Brody's missions took him across the globe, often living in high style. Most of the citizens of his have-not homeland could only dream of that kind of life.

Arriving at the Charlottesville armory near dawn, he found the red brick building swarming with activity. Reservists shuffled in, mustering for service. Military trucks came and went, drawing munitions for their units. As Brody's intelligence division already knew, the virgies were preparing for another war with Pennsylvania. But Brody wasn't interested in the locals. His assignment was to get intel on the toads – the sobriquet Britannics used for anyone from Francia.

Near noon, Brody finally spotted his quarry.

A pair of soldiers in red berets from L'Armée de Francia entered the armory. After a few minutes, a different pair of toads left. When this happened twice over the next twelve hours, Brody was sure. They were guards on a six-hour rotation.

But what were they guarding inside the armory? There was only one way to find out. He'd have to go inside.

| DAY THREE |

PARIS, FRANCIA

Croissant and coffee in hand, I hurried past the pawn shop next to our embassy on Rue De Javel. Only a small brass plaque by the door distinguished the building where I worked from the small stores and apartments along the narrow street.

As always, the embassy's door hinge squeaked when I stepped inside. Something like that would have been fixed at the legation of a developed country. But here, no one bothered.

Not that it mattered.

The foreigners who passed through the doors of Virginia's embassy were always pissants carrying water for someone higher up. Virginia's ambassador to Francia was summoned, not visited.

Entering the reception area lit by flickering fluorescent tubes, I nodded to Eugene, the day-shift security guard. The old man's ebony face widened into a grin. "Good morning, Olivia. I see you're early birding again."

Since taking on the op with the Germans, I usually arrived

before most of my embassy colleagues. A near-empty office made clandestine work easier. If Francia – or Virginia – uncovered my op, I'd likely find myself at the end of a rope. The same fate awaited my comrades in Virginia behind this mission.

"Morning, Eugene," I said, placing my briefcase and breakfast on the track for the security scanner. "Your daughter had her baby yet?"

"Baby girl. Eight pounds," he said beaming. "My daughter said to tell you thanks for the stroller. That was a mighty kind gift."

I touched my brow in a salute before collecting my belongings from the scanner. "Always glad to help a vet." Eugene had served with my father in the last war with Pennsylvania.

Arriving at my cubicle on the second floor, I pulled the laptop from my briefcase and logged into the alumni chat room at the Virginia Military Academy. After opening a private message with my former classmate Dot Blake, I typed: *Are the wedding gifts ready?*

While I waited for her reply, I took a bite of croissant and downed some coffee. Dot and I went way back.

We'd been the only female cadets in our class at VMI. Dot and I became way more than gal pals, though. The brutal training of the school's freshman Rat Line revealed a person's character. You learned who to trust. Dot became the sister I never had. We gave each other private nicknames: Dorothy Leigh Blake turned into Dot. Olivia Jane Braxton became OJ.

Through those ordeals, Dot and I developed a church-like faith in our school's code of honor – and in each other. Still, we were an unlikely pair. I was white and a legacy admission. Dot was black and a civic-group scholarship student. But we were both surprised to find we were distant kin through Thomas Jefferson.

During our first tour in the Army, Dot and I fell in with a handful of idealistic young officers. We called our covert group the Patrick Henry Society. Our dream was to reform the army. We'd all been shocked by the incompetence of so many officers. It didn't take us long to learn these slackers had something in common: They'd been promoted for their politics or high-placed connections.

After I left the army for a foreign service career, I kept in touch with Dot and The Hens. The ideals I shared with these comrades had inspired me to help the German cause. I felt their pain.

My own country of Virginia had gone to war to free itself from England in 1776. Now, the Germans were struggling to liberate themselves from Francia's yoke.

When I asked Dot and The Hens to join the German op, they jumped at the chance. The mission was dry kindling for years of smoldering anger.

I knew most of my colleagues at the embassy would call this operation treason. But I felt loyal to a higher cause. I refused to buy the patriotic horseshit of politicians who sold out the needs of their citizens for another private jet or a new vacation home.

A ping from my laptop announced Dot's reply: *The gifts will ship air freight to Caen.*

Before I could answer, I heard footsteps outside my cubicle and minimized the chat room screen.

"Hey, Eugene tells me you like to come early," Nate Whitley said with a smirk as he stepped into my cube. He then slung his arm over the partition and winked. "I'm available to help you with that any time."

Whitley's crude come-on was no surprise. The new ambassador's aide had been hitting on me since he'd arrived in Paris a few weeks earlier.

"Yeah, I like to come early," I said. "But it depends on who's driving me to work – and you can bet it won't be you, Nate."

Whitley forced a smile. "I like a girl who plays hard to get," he said before retreating down the corridor.

Opening the VMI chat room again, I typed: *You're a beast, Dot. I will let you know when to ship the gifts.*

After closing the connection, I exhaled with relief.

My old comrade Dot Blake was now a high-ranking ordnance officer in the Army of Virginia. And Dot had just confirmed a key piece of our covert op with the Germans. She'd managed to confiscate a half-ton of C-4 explosives from the Army of Virginia to topple the Arc de Triomphe.

CHARLOTTESVILLE, VIRGINIA

After a full day of planning, Brody was ready to make his move.

Just over an hour past the midnight change of the red beret guards, he entered the armory dressed as a First Lieutenant in the Virginia Reserves. Just being caught with the uniform in his luggage was a hanging offense. Still, Brody had used this stunt before.

He spotted the red berets near the end of a hallway off the armory's main assembly area. The enlisted men – one a corporal, the other a private – were slouching against the wall, puffing on vape pens, noses in their smartphones. Between them was a door labeled Storage Unit #4. Brody was relieved to see there were no surveillance cameras. The soldiers' lack of discipline was not surprising. Despite the elite appearance of their red berets, the troops deployed to Virginia were mostly misfits.

Brody was grateful the toads were arrogant enough to put their soldiers' names on their tunics. It made conning them much easier. Britannics couldn't afford that kind of luxury for their ragtag armies. The corporal's name was LeClair. The private was named Guyon. Both had an Ordnance Corps patch with crossed cannons on their sleeves.

"Hello tonight, *monsieurs*," Brody said, approaching the men. Although fluent in French, Brody spoke in a crude pidgin.

The corporal looked up from his phone and grudgingly touched his beret in a salute. "You need something, Lieutenant?" The toads had little respect for officers in the Virginia military – especially when they had Brody's tawny shade of skin.

Brody flashed *The Smile*, a cloying look of subservience Britannics used to play the toads. "Boring duty, no?" he said, pulling a pack of Admirals from his chest pocket. "Smoke?" he asked, tearing the cellophane off the tricolor wrapper.

"Are you rich, Lieutenant?" Guyon said as both soldiers killed their vapes and took a cigarette.

"I have important friends," Brody replied. He knew one of the few things toads liked about duty in Virginia was getting their hands on the pricey, old-school cigarettes. Brody brought out a worn zippo lighter and flicked it to start a flame. As the red berets lit up, he asked, "Will Lyon win the cup?"

"For sure," LeClair said, exhaling a cloud of smoke.

Guyon shook his head. "Marseille will kick their asses – again."

Bataille was always a good icebreaker with Franks. They loved their brutal national game. Hell, Brody liked the game himself. He'd played Bataille in college – and still had the scars to prove it.

"You two want to make bet?" Brody asked, pulling a roll of francs from the pocket of his fatigues. "I give you Lyon and twelve points."

"I'll take some of that action," Guyon said. "How much of your money do you want to lose?"

Brody unrolled four 1000-franc notes and held them up. "Yes?" he asked.

"Wait a minute, Guyon," LeClair said. "I thought you were a big fan of Marseille?"

"I'm a bigger fan of taking this nic's money," Guyon said, laughing.

Brody laughed as well, ignoring the slur.

LeClair looked at his comrade. "You trust this guy to pay up?"

Brody peeled off two of the bills and handed the notes to Guyon. "You hold half the bet," he said. Brody could sense the private was his prime mark. And now the hook was set. They'd already broken one regulation for gambling.

While Guyon was pocketing the cash, Brody said, "Maybe some fun for you two tonight?"

"Fun?" Guyon asked.

"Women," Brody said. "Very pretty," he said, then pulled a phone from his pocket. As the soldiers leaned toward him, Brody showed them a photo of the two femmes he'd retained for the evening. Clad in negligees, the women flashed *The Smile*, just as Brody had directed. "Janelle and Ellen. Very friendly," Brody added.

Finding an officer in Virginia's National Guard working a side gig as a pimp would not surprise these soldiers — Brody was sure of that. A cottage industry had sprouted in Virginia serving the vices of Francia's military advisors. And Guyon knew the drill.

"How much?" Guyon asked.

Brody winked. "Nothing tonight. We make friends, yes?"

"I'll take the brown sugar," Guyon said, pointing to the darker-skinned woman. "Hook us up after our shift at 0600."

"Sorry, no," Brody answered. "Only now. I have Renault van

around the corner on Berkmar Street. Very nice."

"We can't," LeClair protested. "We're on duty."

Brody shrugged. "You go. I stay here," he said, then pointed to the Security Division insignia on his shoulder. "No problem."

The soldiers looked at each other. "I don't think we should," LeClair said.

"LeClair, this LT is in security," Guyon said.

"I know," LeClair replied, "But I'm not sure that makes it right."

Guyon clapped his comrade's shoulder. "Come on, man. This is a free jump. Live a little."

"Well... I suppose..." LeClair said, his voice drifting off.

Guyon grabbed the corporal by the arm. "We're in," he said, pulling LeClair toward the exit.

"Enjoy, my friends," Brody said as the soldiers walked away. "We will do business again, yes?"

"Yeah. Sure thing, bro," Guyon said over his shoulder.

***

LeClair and Guyon looked up and down the street before stepping out of the armory. Not surprisingly, nothing was moving at this hour of the night.

"You got any raincoats on you?" LeClair asked as the pair started down the tree-lined street.

"Son, these women may be nics but they're professionals," Guyon answered. "They'll have more bubble wrap than you'll ever need."

Head swiveling, LeClair said, "You sure we won't get caught?"

"How long have you been in-country, LeClair?"

"Three months."

"I've been in this shithole almost a year. Don't worry. This kind of stuff goes on all the time."

"But you've seen our new Colonel, man. He's trying to play the bad ass. He wants to make his bones busting enlisted men for screwing up."

"That's just a pose to scare you, LeClair. You think the Colonel really wants any of his men on report? That would make *him* look bad."

"Yeah, but I think it's different when it comes to bloom."

"You're wrong, man," Guyon said. "That would make any violations even worse for him."

"God, I hope you're right."

Guyon pulled the bet money from his pocket. "I think this nic pimp is going to be good for—"

"Look!" LeClair said, pointing to headlights approaching on the street. Ducking behind a tree, he said, "Get out of sight, Guyon."

The pair watched from the shadows as two military trucks drove by.

His eyes wide, LeClair said, "Do you think they're headed for the armory?"

"How the hell would I know?"

"I think we should go back."

"Stop being a worm, LeClair. We've got some hot women waiting for us – and they're free."

LeClair shook his head. "If we get caught, they'll lock us up."

"All right," Guyon said. "Then *you* go back. If those trucks brought any nosy officers, tell them I'm in the latrine and call me."

***

Picking the lock on the door to Storage Unit #4 had taken Brody less than a minute once he was sure the red berets had left the armory.

Stepping into a room about five-by-five meters, Brody slowly looked around.

There would be more than enough time to check out the storage space. He'd provided the professional women in the van with oxy-spiked cognac as part of their entertainment. Brody had used demi-mondes in his work before. They were great assets almost everywhere he went – reliable, fearless and discreet.

The only thing in the storage space were two suitcase-sized ordnance crates. Marked only with the number 262-D, the containers looked new, their black plastic skin unscuffed and shiny.

Using his phone, Brody took a picture of the containers, then unsnapped the top crate.

The contents looked familiar – like a load of C4. But the blocks of explosive putty shrink-wrapped in clear plastic were green, not the usual gray or tan. The packages were marked *Munition Biologique*.

"So this is what bloom looks like," he whispered to himself.

For months, Francia's powerful new explosive had been the buzz of intelligence services around the world. Commonly called bloom, *munition biologique* was reported to be six times more powerful than C4 – and was a terrorist's dream. The living compound continually reinvented its own scent, making it impossible to train dogs in detecting it.

And now bloom was here in Virginia – ready to be deployed against Pennsylvania.

After taking another photo, Brody drew a pocketknife and sliced a sample the size of a grain of rice from the bottom of one of the packets. Placing the bloom in the vial he'd brought, he pocketed the evidence and returned the bloom packet to its original spot.

Closing the crate, he heard steps in the hallway. Then the door opened.

When LeClair stepped into the room, Brody asked, "Problem with the women?"

"Never mind that," the soldier answered. "What are you doing in here?"

"I heard noise," Brody answered. "I come to look," he said, pointing to his eye. Then he shrugged and raised his palms. "No trouble."

"How did you get in?"

From his pocket, Brody took out the key to his room at the B&B. "Master key. All security officers have this," he said.

Still wary, LeClair opened the containers and looked inside. "Everything seems fine," he said. "But I'll need to report this."

Brody smiled and touched his temple. "Think, my friend. No problem here," he said, waving his hand around the room. "If you report, bad for *me* and bad for *you*."

LeClair's edge faded as he considered Brody's words. To report this breach of security, the corporal would have to explain to his lieutenant why he'd left his post – and that would probably land him in the stockade.

Brody sensed his message had hit home. "We are friends now. You trust me. I trust you," he said, then pulled out the two 1000-franc notes he'd shown them earlier. "You hold rest of bet," he said, pressing the money into the soldier's hands. "I come get if I win. Yes?"

"That seems fair," LeClair said, putting the money into his pocket.

Brody winked, gave him *The Smile*, and ambled away.

| Day Four |

PHILADELPHIA, PENNSYLVANIA

Brody knocked on the door.

"Come in," a deep voice said from the other side.

Brody entered a room he'd visited many times, always with trepidation.

The director's office at the Security Bureau of the People's Republic of Pennsylvania was windowless and dim. A portrait on the wall of the current Premier offered the only decoration. But this stark room belied the power of its occupant.

Behind a worn wooden desk, Jim Easley removed the unlit cigar from his mouth and pointed it toward the chair in front of him. "Sit down, son," he said to Brody. "You did some fine work in Charlottesville."

"Thanks, boss," Brody answered, settling into the chair.

The furrows on his chief's bronze face deepened. "Can't say I'm happy about what you found, though," Easley said. "The fellas at the lab checked out the sample you brought back. They've never seen anything like it, but they're sure it's bloom. Couldn't be anything else."

"They shouldn't have been surprised. The packages were marked *Munition Biologique*."

"Sure, but the toads can be devious. They might have tried to bullshit the virgies into thinking they had the real deal. The Franks don't trust Britannics – even when they're allies."

"So what are we going to do about the bloom?"

"I've asked the premier to authorize a raid on the armory."

Brody's eyebrows rose. "Boss, a raid on the armory will start another war with Virginia."

"I know that. But we can't allow the virgies to use that batch of bloom against us. Their agents could slip into any of our cities and take out a block with a chunk of explosives the size of a candy bar – and there's no way we can detect it. We'll never have enough security people to protect all the possible targets." Easley said. "If we're going to war, I'd rather it starts with our raid on that armory instead of the virgies leveling one of our cities."

"Taking out the bloom in Charlottesville won't keep the toads from sending more."

"You're right, son," Easley said. "We need to shut down the pipeline of bloom into Virginia."

"How are we going to do that?"

"The toads will do it for us," Easley said. "Francia's prime minister has an election coming up. He's already having trouble drumming up public support for his decision to send military advisors to Virginia. If word gets out that he's giving bloom to the virgies, the opposition party will accuse him of promoting terrorism and run his ass out of office."

"So the toads want to keep the bloom in Virginia a secret."

"Exactly. And that's where you come in," the chief said. "I'm sending you to Paris with an unlimited per diem. Your job there is to find out who's responsible for sending the bloom to Virginia. Once we have their names, we can leak it to the media. When news about the bloom breaks, the opposition party in Francia will do the rest."

"You sure this will work, boss?"

"The media can be a weapon, son. Never forget that."

"Even with a carte blanche, getting those names won't be easy."

"It gets even harder," Easley said. "You've got forty-eight hours. If I don't hear from you before that, we'll launch the raid on the armory. You're our long shot to stop the war, son. Don't fuck it up."

1785

PHILADELPHIA, PENNSYLVANIA

Striding past the stately homes along Philadelphia's
Market Street, Thomas Paine was dismayed.
The residents of this affluent district still lived
comfortably. The rest of the city – along with most
of the nation Paine had labored to establish – was
another matter entirely.

In the four years since Pennsylvania had won its
independence from England, the euphoria of victory
had withered into despair for most citizens. When
Paine had written Common Sense – a widely-read
manifesto demanding liberty – he had never imagined
an outcome like this.

Pennsylvania's new national government was
heavily in debt from the war and forced to raise taxes.
Farmers had rebelled. Shopkeepers were losing money.
Inflation was rampant. Soldiers who had fought in
Pennsylvania's war of independence had stormed the

General Assembly demanding to be paid for their service during the war. The rebellion was suppressed by troops loyal to President John Dickinson.

There was only one bright spot. The peace with the Shawnee and Seneca settlements was holding.

Despite that, the troubling chain of events across the country had led Paine to a dark conclusion: Without bold action, financial ruin would destroy the democratic ideals that had inspired Pennsylvania's independence.

But Paine had a plan that would restore justice and prosperity to their young nation.

Today, he would visit a man who had helped found their nation, a man whose genius spanned science, philosophy and politics, perhaps the only man with the wisdom and the will to save the nation... his mentor, Benjamin Franklin.

Paine had idolized the older Franklin from the time they'd met eleven years earlier. The two had remained close friends ever since.

The familiar face of Franklin's negro butler Peter greeted Paine at the door. "We've been expecting you, sir," he said, waving him inside. "Master Ben said to bring you straight into his study."

Entering the study, Paine found the septuagenarian puttering at a large table strewn with Leyden jars, woodworking tools and a chess set. Behind Franklin were floor to ceiling bookshelves fronted by a pair of chairs. Tall windows on two walls flooded the space with light.

Paine bowed his head respectfully. "Very kind of you to receive me so soon after your return, sir." Franklin had been in Paris for the last four years.

Extending his palm, Franklin smiled and said,

"Glad to see you again, Tom. You look no worse for wear."

"I wish I could say the same for our nation," Paine said, shaking his mentor's hand.

"Still not one for small talk, I see," Franklin said, gesturing toward the chairs. "Please, sit." The old man then addressed his butler. "Mister Paine and I will have tea, Peter."

Once the servant was out of the room, the men settled into their chairs.

"I fear last year's mutiny in Philadelphia was a warning sign, sir," Paine said.

"You're not the first to remind me, Tom. I doubt you'll be the last."

"Our nation calls itself a commonwealth. But Pennsylvania is not living up to its founding principles. We promised to provide for the common good of our people. The rebellion by our troops proves we're failing at that."

"Providing for the common good doesn't mean granting every request from our citizens. We must be prudent."

"Where does prudence end and greed begin, sir? Most of the men who led our independence from England were already rich burghers and landholders. They protected their wealth from London's high-handed taxes. But what about the common man of Pennsylvania? What has he gained through our revolution from England?"

Franklin nodded. "I'll admit, the conditions you've observed influenced my decision to return from France. But why come to me, Tom? I have no official role in the government."

"You've earned the respect of the

Constitutionalists and the Republicans in the General Assembly, sir. They'll stop bickering and listen to you."

"I'm not sure what I can say to persuade either party."

Paine pulled a small tin box from his pocket and opened the lid. "Would you care for some snuff, sir?"

"No, thank you."

Paine placed a pinch of the cured tobacco on the back of his hand, brought it to his nose and inhaled. "This snuff is from the Jefferson plantation in Virginia. I'm told it's favored by the finest houses in Europe."

"Yes, that's true. But I find snuff a useless indulgence."

"Hard to argue with your assessment, sir. However, the tobacco growers in Virginia profit handsomely by exporting their crop. Pennsylvania's exports of wheat and other foodstuff are nowhere near as profitable."

"Our soil and climate are not favorable to growing tobacco."

"Exactly. We have fewer cash crops. That leaves our treasury weak and hard pressed to fund the common good we both support."

"New York has the same soil and climate. Why are they not suffering as much?"

"That's one of the changes we've seen in your absence. Despite Hamilton's resistance, New York City has become a haven for foreign smugglers and usurious banking. We have not stooped to that sort of chicanery in Pennsylvania."

A middle-aged woman entered the room carrying a silver tray with a teapot, sugar and biscuits. "Where would you like your tea, Master Ben?" the negro servant asked.

"On the table will be fine, Jemima," Franklin answered. "We'll serve ourselves," he said, then flicked his fingers, dismissing her.

Paine rose and walked to the table. "As I said, sir, we lack the wealth to provide for the needs of the common man. But I think there may be a solution."

"I'm open to hearing it."

"Follow the example of Adams in Massachusetts," Paine said, filling two cups with tea. "Consolidate the wealth of our region."

Franklin's eyebrows rose. "Are you proposing we annex our neighbors?"

Two years earlier, troops under the command of President Samuel Adams of Massachusetts had seized control of New Hampshire, Connecticut, and Rhode Island in a bloodless takeover.

Paine handed his mentor a cup of tea. "I think liberate is a more appropriate term than annex. The tobacco growers in Virginia, Delaware and Maryland exploit the free labor of negroes to live in luxury. Our intervention would bring justice to those nations. More importantly, it would give us the wealth to promote the welfare of the common man, as we've always dreamed."

"How would we raise an army? We still owe the soldiers who fought in the war against England."

"We can pay them with free land in the new territory we acquire. I believe many of them would jump at the chance."

"Taking on three nations would be reckless, Tom. Virginia alone can match our population of free citizens."

"We don't need to eat the apple in one bite," Paine said, handing Franklin a cup of tea. "The tobacco plantations in Maryland and Delaware would boost our wealth considerably. And we outnumber the free people of both nations combined."

"Tobacco is a voracious crop," Franklin said. "It depletes the soil and forces its growers to constantly seek new land."

"By the time the soil gives out for tobacco, we'll have our fiscal house in order. Our farmers will grow new crops on the same soil," Paine said. "You'll have a larger territory for your personal experiments with new plants and farming, sir."

"What about the negro slaves who work the plantations? What do you propose to do with them once the soil gives out?"

"After the brutal toil of the fields, they'll be happy to work as domestic servants. Your household is proof of that."

Rubbing his chin, Franklin said, "Even if some remain in the fields, negro labor in rural areas might discourage more Germans from coming here. The blacks at least speak English and follow our customs."

"I'm delighted you're realizing the possibilities of this proposal, sir."

Franklin shook his head. "I still find conquest an unsavory business."

"As do I, sir. But we fought England for a just cause. I believe it's time to take up arms for the common good again. We face another desperate situation."

"The military preparations would need to be kept secret if this enterprise is to have any chance of success," Franklin said, adding sugar to his tea.

"That's why you would be the perfect person to propose it. I can arrange for you to meet privately with the party leaders of the General Assembly."

After taking a sip of tea, Franklin said, "I see no harm in meeting with them."

"You're stepping to the fore as a champion of the people once again, sir," Paine said beaming. "With your help, we'll strengthen the foundation of a government that will always strive for the good of the common man."

***

Less than two miles away, in a commercial district of the city, Elizabeth Ross looked up from her sewing as the bell above the door rang.

"Good afternoon, Betsy," her client, Edna Marsh, said entering the upholstery shop.

Betsy put down the quilt she was stitching and stood. "Good afternoon, Mrs. Marsh. It's very good to see you again," she said, trying to contain her excitement. This was the first customer to enter Betsy's shop in more than a week.

"I'd like some new curtains for our drawing room," the wealthy matron said. "We'll be receiving guests next month. Can you manage two sets that quickly?"

Betsy tapped her fingers together. "Yes, I should think so," she said nodding. In fact, she had no other commissions. "Do you know what length and width you'll need?"

"Yes," Edna said, handing Betsy a piece of paper from her reticule. "I had our butler take the measurements."

"Shall we look at some fabric samples?" Betsy said, guiding her customer to a counter with swatches of cloth bound into a book.

Within a half-hour Mrs. Marsh had made her decision. She would have cream chintz curtains with red trim.

"I'll have your drapes ready in two weeks, Mrs. Marsh," Betsy said as her client left the shop.

White chintz Betsy had aplenty in her shop's stock of fabrics. But red. Ah, red was dear these days. In better times, she would have ordered the fabric from a merchant. However, with business scarce and profits rare, finding some leftover scraps of red cloth seemed a wiser choice.

Walking into the back room, Betsy knelt before a wooden chest and opened the lid. Near the bottom of a trunk filled with remnants from previous commissions, Betsy found what she was looking for.

The sight of the red, white and blue flag in her hands brought back a flood of memories.

Nine years ago, a delegate from Virginia to the Continental Congress had come to see her and commissioned the flag. She couldn't recall the man's name but his idea seemed mad: joining all the colonies into a single nation.

Still, she'd taken the job. He'd given her four pounds sterling in advance and promised four more when she'd finished the flag.

The Virginian never returned and Betsy soon forgot him as the war against the British started.

Her husband joined the militia and was killed a few months later. But she barely had time to grieve John. The war kept her busy making blankets and tents, repairing uniforms and even stuffing paper cartridges with powder and musket balls.

Yes, she'd been busy. But like so many others, the government had only paid for a fraction of her work.

Now, everyone was owed money they'd never see. Worse still, there were few prospects for new business. Who would have expected that independence from the king's taxes would bring another form of misery?

Betsy sighed. Then she carried the flag to her workbench, pulled a seam ripper from a drawer and began taking apart the red, white and blue fabric.

~=~

| Day Five |

PARIS, FRANCIA

The verge on Rue de Bièvre was like most in the 17th Arrondissement, a weedy strip of grass and trees hugging a street lined with beige, five-story buildings. Seated on a bench in that greenspace, Brody faked a call on his mobile while he cased an apartment building a half-block away. Near him, his electric motorbike was parked along the curb.

From the pocket of his leather jacket, Brody uncapped a bottle of benzies and gulped his third pill of the day. The flight across the pond had left him little time for sleep. Forty-eight hours ago he'd been in Philly, briefing his boss on the op in Charlottesville.

After arriving in Paris, Brody had stopped at their safehouse in Montmartre to drop off his suitcase and pick up a Glock, 250,000 francs and an identity as Hassan Rashid. His snooping had started at Virginia's embassy. His mole at the embassy – nurtured over several sultry stints in Paris – had led him to Olivia Braxton.

As the embassy's military liaison officer, Braxton would likely know how Francia was supplying the bloom to Virginia. So tailing her became his first priority.

When Brody saw Braxton leave her apartment building, he donned his helmet and raised the kickstand on his motorbike. A wise decision, it turned out.

In less than a minute, she entered an eCAB and headed east on Rue de Bièvre. Brody gunned the motorbike's mute electric engine, keeping the eCAB in sight from a block behind. Weaving perilously through the snarl of slow-moving cars, he prayed no one opened a door.

Braxton got out of the car at the Gustave Moreau Museum and entered the building. Sightseeing? According to her dossier, she'd been in Paris several years. Braxton was likely being wary. On a hunch, he drove around the block.

There she was, coming out of an alley.

Brody drove by, keeping an eye on her in the rearview mirror. Pulling beside a parked pickup, he stopped and watched her through the truck's window as she walked into a sports bar. Undoubtedly packed with patrons for today's Bataille match, a noisy bar might be a good site for a clandestine meeting. After a few minutes, Brody followed her inside.

***

A thick cloud of smoke hung near the ceiling of the sports bar as I walked inside. On more than a dozen plasma screens, a gray-haired man in a lab coat appeared.

"What do you vape, Doctor?" a voice-over announcer asked.

"I vape HaleBreez," the doctor said, smiling. " It's the only brand of tobacco scientifically proven to protect your throat against irritation and—"

Ignoring the rest of the spiel, I slid into an empty booth along the wall. The place was filling up fast. In a few minutes, the Bataille match between Marseille and Lyon would begin.

I hated the fucking sport.

It wasn't the violence that bothered me. No, it was watching two armor-clad teams advancing on a lined field in military formations – a crass spectacle celebrating Francia's culture of conquest.

Despite my disdain for Bataille, the crowded bar was a good spot for a meet up.

After firing up an e-cig, I took a long drag and glanced at the time on my burner. My contact with the Germans, Ludolph Eltz, was late.

Had he missed the dead drop signal?

To appease Ludolph's paranoia, I had agreed to place a pair of stones near the entrance to Parc Poyet whenever I needed to meet with him. I would then leave a message with the time and place to meet under a particular trash bin in the park.

Most likely, Ludolph was holding a grudge and making me wait. He'd not taken my brush off to his latest advances too well.

I'd met Eltz at an embassy reception shortly after being assigned to duty in Paris. At first, I'd dismissed his potential as an ally. Eltz seemed more interested in a horizontal romp. But as we talked over several embassy soirees, his grievances against Francia changed my mind. A member of the German separatist party, the Freedom Coalition, Ludolph shared my loathing of the Franks – and that had sown the seeds of our alliance.

Still, fending him off was tiresome. I'd endured men like Eltz and Whitley during my career as a soldier and a diplomat. They saw women lower on the pecking order as fair game for their come ons.

I'd always kept my wardrobe prim and makeup minimal. My

hair was cut simply, in a medium length. Long hair was a magnet for some men. Very short hair was a turn-on as well, I'd discovered – usually for someone creepy. Despite my deterrents, Eltz had become one more in a long line of Don Juan wannabes.

I motioned for the waiter and ordered another Pernod.

Being deployed to Paris was a plum assignment for a diplomat from the Britannic region. Daily life was grim in the English-speaking nations of North America.

Fortunately for me, I had the kind of looks that vaulted you to the top of Virginia's duty list for Francia. My fair skin, green eyes and honey blonde hair made me indistinguishable from most white Parisians. The same did not hold true for many of my countrymen. Like all Britannic nations, Virginia reflected its history in the phenotypes of its people. I could not deny the harsh reality of my country. We were a pigmentocracy where the minority of English origin held sway over a majority of African and indigenous ancestry.

The opening strains of *La Marseillaise* silenced all conversation in the bar. Over one-hundred patrons rose as one and began to sing. Not wanting to attract attention, I joined them.

On the broadcast, a perfectly timed flyover of the stadium by L'Armée de l'Air jets at the end of the anthem brought a roar from the crowd. The camera zoomed to a group of soldiers in red berets waving to the other fans in the stadium. "We're proud to honor our military advisors serving with distinction in Virginia!" shouted the stadium announcer. As the cheers rose again, I fought the urge to hurl my drink at the screen.

These fucking toads weren't in Virginia to help my country. Francia planned to use Virginia as a test lab for their latest weapons.

Another war between Virginia and Pennsylvania looked likely.

Politicians in both nations were once again saber-rattling over their disputed border at the headwaters of the Potomac. It was an old trick. The real motive was to spread a patriotic fever and distract people from the relentless misery in both nations.

But this time, many more Virginians would die than in our previous wars with the pennies. I'd learned from Dot that Francia was secretly supplying deadly new weapons like *munitions biologique* to the Army of Virginia.

In response, the Soviets had increased their shipments of arms to Pennsylvania. Through the corruption and vanity of our own leaders, Virginia and Pennsylvania would soon be pawns in a proxy war between the superpowers.

I'd lost my father and a brother to the last war with Pennsylvania. And for what?

Most people in Virginia and the other Britannic nations still lived in poverty. We lagged behind the developed world in literacy, wages and life expectancy. We lived in corrupt, volatile countries wracked by coups and exploited by more powerful nations. And we were all reviled with the same epithet... nics.

There were others in Virginia who shared my anger. Not many, for sure. Most of my allies were young and educated. They were fortunate enough to see beyond the daily struggle for survival that blinded most of our countrymen to the injustice around them.

There was more than idealism in my alliance with the Germans, though. A separatist uprising within Francia's borders would draw the toads' military away from the Britannic region. That would save lives back home.

A roar rose in the bar as Lyon won the first Skirmish. Scanning the room again, I finally saw Ludolph Eltz making his way toward my table. Short and jowly with a gray combover, Ludolph's sleek track suit seemed a vain choice for his pudgy frame.

Eltz sneered as he slipped into the booth. "A sports bar? Your taste in meeting sites should not surprise me."

I sighed. Clearly, he was still smarting from my latest rebuff. "This is a secure location, Ludolph. No way the toads can bug us here," I said waving toward the noisy screens around us.

"Toads?"

"It's something Britannics call the Franks."

"What a dazzling wit you people have," he said with a sour smile.

"Look, Ludolph. I can see you're upset. But I need to make this clear. Nothing is going to happen between us. There's too much at stake for this to become personal." Even if I'd found Ludolph attractive, I'd already had one fling with a fellow diplomat in Paris. It ended badly.

"Your country may be in the New World, but your prudish attitudes are passé."

"I doubt your wife would agree."

"Ah, but that's where you're wrong, my dear," Eltz said. "She pursues her own interests."

I can certainly understand why, I wanted to say. Instead, I said, "Let's focus on our mission."

"Fine," he said curtly.

"Have your tactical people finally decided how much C4 they'll need?" As a former artillery officer, I knew demolishing a structure the size of the Arc de Triomphe was no mean feat.

"We don't want C4. We want bloom."

"My asset in Virginia only has access to conventional ordnance. The toads keep a round-the-clock guard on their new weapon."

"My colleagues insist on bloom."

"Why?"

"Think of the statement it will make," Eltz said, stroking the back of his hand. "On the anniversary of Frederick the Great's coronation, Francia will see its cherished monument destroyed with its own secret weapon. Their humiliation will ignite our cause."

I shook my head. "Bloom is off the table. It's too risky."

"My colleagues warned me you would say that," Eltz said with a smirk. "They say nics lack the spycraft to crack Francia's security. Maybe they are right."

I rose from the table. "I've had enough of your shit, Eltz. Get your own goddam fireworks," I said, gathering my purse and cellphone.

"Wait. Wait," Eltz said, lifting his palm. "I have been rude. Please sit down."

After a long sigh, I slipped back into the booth.

Eltz smiled. "I'm a cranky old man and I sometimes forget there are still Aryans like you in the Britannic countries. You don't deserve to be lumped with the crossbreeds. Please don't take offense. My criticism was never directed at *you*. During our alliance, you have displayed nothing but honor and courage."

Despite myself, I felt a trace of pride. "All right. I'll accept your apology – but only because we have a common enemy. Understand?"

"Of course," Eltz answered, bowing slightly. "Our mission is too important."

Satisfied with his contrition, I said, "We have five days until your target date. If we're going to get the ordnance on time, the shipment from Virginia needs to get underway *now*."

"I understand, my dear. We are most grateful for all you have done for our cause," he said, then added, "May I beg a favor?"

I sighed. "What's the favor?"

"Would you at least ask your asset about the bloom? If there's any chance—"

"I'll ask," I said, interrupting him. "No guarantees." I knew getting the bloom was hopeless. But I felt honor-bound to exhaust every possibility.

"Thank you. How long will you need?"

"Meet me here tomorrow at nine."

Ludolph winced. "Can we meet somewhere else?"

"Is *Le Velours Bleu* pretentious enough for you?"

"Ah, you can be so charming, my dear," Eltz said with an oily smile. "I will see you there tomorrow," he said before leaving the bar.

A loud voice from the televisions drew my attention.

An auto dealer in blackface makeup and a feathered headband was shouting into the camera. "I'm selling cars made in Francia at Britannic prices!" he yelled, faking a thick foreign accent. "Come and make me a deal, paleface!"

I tried not to wince. I'd witnessed racist bullshit like this almost every day I'd been in Francia. In one variation or another, the message was always the same. Everything Britannic was cheap and inferior, the work of mongrel bumpkins.

I finished my Pernod and walked out of the bar.

Civilians might die at the Arc de Triomphe, I reminded myself, heading back to my apartment. Fuck them. The toads have it coming.

***

As Brody surveyed the scene in the sports bar, his decision to tail Braxton looked promising.

She was in a booth and had ordered a drink. After finding a spot at the bar where he could keep eyes on her, Brody lit an Admiral and asked the barman for an Irish coffee.

His target's dossier photo did not do her justice. From the vanilla layer of Virginia's racial parfait, she was tall and fair. As a stunner trying to play it down, Braxton had dressed to blend in.

She ignored the pregame coverage on the televisions and kept glancing at her phone. Whoever she was meeting was late.

Just as Lyon won the first skirmish, Braxton was joined by a male in his mid-fifties who favored a dumpling with a combover. Brody pegged him for a Nordic.

There was no hope of overhearing them, but the conversation between the pair did not look friendly. At one point, Braxton rose and gathered her things. But the dumpling coaxed her back. A few minutes later, the man rose to leave.

Walking toward the entrance, Brody arrived first and placed himself by the door. Faking a phone call as the dumpling walked by, Brody took the man's photo with the custom side lens on his mobile.

After a few minutes, Braxton left the bar.

Tailing Braxton on his motorbike, Brody followed his mark back to her flat. Anticipating a long stakeout, he had rented a Citroen and parked it within sight of her apartment building.

***

Back at my apartment, I poured out an inch of Pernod and sat down at my desk. I was certain asking Dot about the bloom was a waste of time. She'd made it clear the toads were guarding it 24/7. But, like a fool, I'd smoothed Eltz.

I fired up the laptop and logged into the alumni chat room at VMI.

"Shit," I muttered as a pop-up appeared on the screen:

[TEMPORARILY OUT OF SERVICE]

There was no telling how long this breakdown might last. Virginia's technology infrastructure was notoriously fickle. That left me with a hard decision.

The Germans planned to destroy the Arc de Triomphe in six days. Shipping the explosives by air freight would take three to four. Every day I waited for the VMI forum to get back online increased the chances of missing the strike date. There was only one alternative: Call Dot on my burner.

But that was risky.

The burner used DES encryption. That might be enough to foil any toads monitoring foreign calls. Then again, it might not. I'm not a tech geek – but I am a risk taker when the situation calls for it.

Using my government-issued smartphone was out of the question. Although it was encrypted against foreign snooping, the Virginia Security Agency could access my texts and phone conversations – along with their recipients. That's why I always left my smartphone at home when meeting with Eltz. The device gave away my movements.

I pulled the burner from my purse and stared at the phone. It was just after suppertime in Richmond, a good time to call.

God damn that, German. I'd given him my word.

I dialed Dot's number.

***

The Deputy of Surveillance at the Paris SS bureau walked along the row of security specialists monitoring their computers and stopped at the last cubicle.

"You have something for me, Maurice?"

"Sir, our AI monitoring flagged a suspicious call on a burner from a member of the Virginia embassy in Paris," the specialist said, then handed his boss a headset. "I think you'll want to hear this conversation. I've edited the call down to the relevant section."

The deputy put on the headset. "Play it," he said.

Speaking in English, a woman's voice said, *"Sorry to contact you by phone."*

Another female answered. *"I'm sure you've got a good reason. What's up?"*

"They want bloom. Any chance you can get it?"

"Not unless you want to do some wet work."

"No. Casualties will draw attention."

"You still want the regular material?"

"Yeah, ship it. I'll talk some sense into them."

"Okay. How much will they need?"

"You know the objective. Send them more than enough."

"Same carrier and destination?"

"No reason to change that."

"Roger. The goods should be there in three to four days."

The deputy put down the headset. "Who made the call?"

The specialist pulled up a dossier on his screen. "Olivia Braxton. She made the call from her flat in the 17th arrondissement using DES encryption."

"DES? We're not dealing with professionals here. Who did Braxton call?"

"All I have right now is a cellphone in Virginia. It might take days to track down the owner. Those nic telecom systems are a mess."

"Good work, Maurice," the deputy said, patting the tech's shoulder. "Let me know when you've got that location in Virginia."

"What do you make of it, sir?"

"I'll kick this upstairs. Any talk of bloom is going to get their attention."

***

As he waited in the car outside Braxton's apartment for her next move, Brody finally found time to learn the dumpling's identity. Logging into his agency's database through his phone, he uploaded the man's photo.

The results left Brody puzzled.

The dumpling's name was Ludolph Eltz, a high-ranking member of a German separatist group called the Freedom Coalition. Was this guy somehow connected to the pipeline of bloom to the virgies?

Brody needed to learn what was happening here – and fast. The raid on the Charlottesville armory was less than 36 hours away. Once that happened, Virginia would almost certainly declare war on the PRP – and security in Paris would get tighter than an ice swimmer's nutsack. His only advantage was that the virgies were unaware his side knew about the bloom.

He'd need to keep an eye on Braxton round the clock. That meant finding a way to get some sleep. From the contacts on his mobile, Brody placed a call.

"Hello, *mon cœur*," a woman's voice said.

"Are you free tonight, Eva?"

"I'll always make time for you."

"Wonderful," he said, then gave her the address where he was parked.

When Eva arrived, Brody lowered the car window and motioned

the red-haired escort inside.

Eva's eyebrows rose. "This is not your style, *mon cœur*," she said getting into the rented Citroën.

Brody smiled. "It's not what you think, *ma chérie*," he said, then showed Eva a photo on his mobile. "I need to get some sleep. Wake me up if you see this woman come out of that building tonight."

1788

MONTICELLO, VIRGINIA

The butler tapped twice on the door frame and waited.

Composing a letter at his desk, Thomas Jefferson finished the sentence he'd started before looking up. "Yes, Colbert?" he finally said.

"Mister Washington has arrived and is waiting in the parlor, Sir," the elegantly dressed servant announced. Unlike the other enslaved workers owned by Jefferson, Colbert's duties as butler granted him special privileges.

Jefferson turned his eyes back to the letter. "Tell him I'll be there directly."

Let him wait, Jefferson thought. *Washington will be much less contentious if I make it clear his station is no longer as high.*

Yes, much to Jefferson's delight, their fortunes had reversed since the Second Continental Congress.

Lionized as the commander of the Continental Army during the war with England, Washington seemed destined to become Virginia's first head of state. But George's ham-fisted diplomacy during the truce with England cooled the public ardor. The presidency had gone to the revolutionary war firebrand, Patrick Henry. Washington had hastened his own fall from grace by using the press to petulantly attack his detractors in the new House of Delegates.

Meanwhile, Jefferson had experienced an epiphany. After being spurned in his quest for unity in 1776, he learned a valuable lesson. It was more effective to redirect the currents of his peers than to swim against them. Using the hefty profits from his plantation as leverage, he'd risen to become chairman of the Appropriations Committee in the Virginia House of Delegates. And that's why Washington was here today. Jefferson was certain of that.

After carefully putting away his quill, he strolled from his study to the parlor.

Washington rose from his chair as Jefferson entered the room. "Thank you for seeing me, sir," he said with a nod.

"You're always welcome at Monticello, George," Jefferson said, waving for him to sit. "Virginia owes you so much."

"I'm glad to hear that because I'm here to collect on that debt," Washington said, settling back into a chair.

As usual, George has the subtlety of a sledgehammer, thought Jefferson. "I take that to mean military appropriations," he said aloud, sitting down across from him.

"Your committee has rejected my request for military aid to Maryland and Delaware – twice."

"George, you're always welcome in my home as a guest. We're Tidewater people. But as a general in the Army of Virginia, coming here to discuss legislative budgets is highly irregular, wouldn't you say?"

"Don't try to hide behind protocol, sir. We don't have time for that," Washington said tersely. "The Pennsylvanians are planning to invade Maryland and Delaware. We need to help them with weapons and supplies. Paine and his gang in Philadelphia are taking a page from Sam Adams."

"I don't think what happened in Massachusetts is the same at all."

"Why not?"

"The nations Adams occupied were sympathetic to his cause. They all went to war with England to stop the embargo of their goods. You know that, George."

"They were united at the start of the war, I agree. But once Adams was given liberty to move his troops into New Hampshire, Connecticut and Rhode Island, he used them to take control of his neighbors after the British signed the peace treaty."

"There was never any bloodshed."

"It would have been futile for them to resist. Adams had superior forces – and they were already entrenched in every capital."

"That's a matter of opinion, George," Jefferson said, waving his hand dismissively.

"It's not an opinion that New Hampshire, Connecticut and Rhode Island are no longer sovereign nations. They all call Boston their capital now."

"By choice, George. They formed a union for the common good."

"With Sam Adams as their permanent head of state," Washington said, rolling his eyes. "How fortunate for him."

Jefferson sighed. "I'm afraid our opinions will remain unresolved on this issue."

"Even if conditions were different in Massachusetts, one fact remains, sir. If we lose Maryland and Delaware as allies, Pennsylvania will take control of Chesapeake Bay."

"I think you're overstating the risk. Virginia has shared the bay with neighboring nations for nearly three decades. I don't see the threat."

"Maryland and Delaware use negroes to work their plantations, just as we do. That will change if Pennsylvania takes control. Don't you see? This is a threat to our way of life."

Jefferson crossed his arms. "What I see quite clearly is the opinion of my constituents. They're not ready to pay more in taxes to protect Maryland and Delaware. They both compete with us in selling tobacco to Europe. The president and most of the House agree. It's as simple as that, George."

Washington stood and walked to the door. Before leaving the parlor, he turned to Jefferson and said, "You're making a grave mistake, sir. Our nation will suffer the consequences."

~=~

| Day Six |

PARIS, FRANCIA

"She's leaving," Eva said, nudging Brody with her elbow.

Brody opened his eyes, squinted at the morning sun and yawned. "Thank you," he said. From the wallet in his jacket, Brody counted out double Eva's usual rate and handed her the bills.

Eva smiled. "The old-fashioned way would have been much more fun, *mon cœur*."

"Next time, Eva. I promise," he said as she stepped out of the car.

Turning his gaze toward Braxton, Brody watched as she joined the stream of morning commuters walking along the street. He knew where she was headed. Her embassy was six blocks away, an easy walk in good weather like this. Once she turned the corner, Brody started the car. Minutes later, he was parked near Braxton's embassy, waiting for her to arrive.

Virginia's consulate was not imposing. Like most buildings in Paris, the four-story embassy was pressed against its neighbors on both sides – a pawn shop and a laundry. The rest of the backwater street was lined with small shops and apartments.

For the rest of the day, Brody watched the doorway, changing locations to avoid being detected. Seven hours and two packs of Admirals later, he was in a coffee shop with a view of the embassy door hunched over a laptop, posing as a remote worker. Instead of seeing Braxton leave the embassy, Brody got an ugly surprise.

A black Peugeot with two men in dark suits pulled into a parking space with a sight line to the embassy door. There was no doubt they were SS.

What had drawn the toad agents here? Was Braxton involved?

The answer came when Brody saw Olivia emerge from the embassy.

As Braxton began her walk toward home, one of the SS men left the car and melted into the procession of homeward workers on the sidewalk. She was being tailed.

This would make his own tail on Braxton harder. With the SS following her, Brody would have to stay undetected by both. His best move for now would be to follow the toads. Fortunately, he knew where they were headed.

***

Arriving at Braxton's apartment behind the wheel of his rental, Brody spotted the black Peugeot parked nearby. Both SS agents were inside. Although he could not see the door to Olivia's apartment building, the toads' presence told him Braxton was in her apartment. After finding a parking spot where he could observe the SS agents, Brody hunkered down to wait.

The clock on the dash of his Citroen read 8:07 when the SS agents started their car and drove away from Braxton's apartment. Brody followed them, careful with his shadowing. The SS men were professionals.

Less than ten-minutes later, the black Peugeot pulled to the curb along a side street off Avenue des Champs-Élysées. Brody drove past the SS car. Stopping might have given him away. Further up the block, he saw Olivia Braxton on the sidewalk in a black dress and spike heels.

Brody pulled over and watched through the rearview mirror as she entered a night club. A chichi sign above the door read: *Le Velours Bleu*.

The lights on the black Peugeot came on. From their parking spot along the street, the SS vehicle pulled into an alley next to the night club. Brody then saw one of the SS men appear on the sidewalk and enter the front door of *Le Velours Bleu*. Their intent was unmistakable. One man was entering through the back door, another through the front.

The SS agents were moving in for an arrest.

***

I hated spike heels. They were absurd, cumbersome and painful. All the same, I'd put on a patent leather pair with the black dress I picked for my meet up with Eltz tonight. A woman in flats and slacks would draw attention at *Le Velours Bleu*.

Eltz was already at a table near the back when I walked into the dimly lit night club. The place was bustling with the typical nobs in these relics from the 20th century. As usual for an older crowd, the scent of menthol-laced tobacco hung in the air.

My call to Dot last night had cleared my conscience. I could assure Eltz the bloom was a no-go.

"What will you have to drink?" Ludolph asked as I sat down across from him. Unlike the sports bar, Eltz looked at ease here.

"Nothing," I said, putting my purse on the table. "I don't have much time." I wanted to quash any thoughts he might have of making this meeting more than it was.

"I hope you bring good news," Eltz said, leaning toward her.

"Yes. Your shipment of C4 is on its way to Caen."

"That is unacceptable," Eltz said, his face flushing. "This is more than an attack, my dear. It is a political statement. We must use bloom."

"If you want to make a statement, why not launch your attack on Bastille Day? Media from all over the world will be there covering the parade."

"That is ridiculous. The security preparations would make that impossible."

"Oh? Yet you won't accept my word when I tell you the same thing," I said. "Look, Ludolph. I took a risk calling on a burner last night to ask for your fucking bloom. The answer was no. Let's move on."

"It is a shame that someone with your beauty and intelligence was raised in a tobacco republic that breeds such small minds."

I was about to answer when I noticed a tall man in a dark suit enter the bar and gaze across the room. He was SS, I was sure.

As a precaution, I checked out an escape route through the back. *Shit.* Another SS goon was coming through the kitchen door.

Stay calm, I told myself as the men walked closer. Maybe they're after someone else.

The taller of the SS agents gripped my arm and lifted me out of the chair. "You'll need to come with us," he said, taking my purse from the table. He then nodded toward Eltz and spoke to his partner. "Take him as well."

"Whatever this is, you are mistaken," Eltz said as he was

dragged out of his chair. "I barely know this woman."

"You can explain it at headquarters," the tall agent said as they hustled us toward the rear exit.

The other patrons kept their eyes down, fearful of being caught up in the raid.

***

When Brody saw the SS agent enter the front door of the night club, his heart began to pound. He could not let them take Braxton into custody. She was his only lead into the bloom pipeline. If he failed, the slaughter of his countrymen was inevitable.

Brody drew his Glock, chambered a round, and returned the gun to his pocket. He'd need to get close to take out the SS men without harming Braxton.

Stepping out of the car, he made his way past the door of the night club and peered down the alley beside it. About fifteen paces down the garbage-strewn passageway, the SS agents were trying to get Braxton and Eltz into the back of the Peugeot. Braxton was putting up a hell of a fight.

Spotting an empty wine bottle in the debris, Brody picked it up and began staggering toward them. "Hey, what are you doing to that lady?" he slurred in French.

"Get out of here before you get hurt, you drunken idiot. We're SS," said the agent holding Braxton by the hair. His partner had a grip on the arm of Ludolph Eltz.

"Yeah? Lemme see your badges," Brody said, shuffling closer.

Still wrestling with Braxton, the agent holding her said, "Shoot this asshole, Claude."

When Claude reached for his weapon, Brody swung the bottle, striking him in the face. While Claude went down, Brody grabbed the agent tussling with Braxton. As the agent turned his attention to Brody, Braxton landed a kick to the SS man's groin.

Drawing his Glock, Brody finished the agents with two shots.

Gasping for breath, her hair disheveled, Braxton looked at Brody. "Who are you?"

"A friend," he answered in French. "Come with me."

Braxton looked around. "Where did he go, the man who was with me?"

"He must have run away. We can't stay here."

"Where's my purse?" she asked, scanning the pavement.

"We don't have time. The gunfire is going to draw a crowd. C'mon."

Carrying her heels in her hand, Braxton followed him.

With Brody leading, the pair walked calmly until they reached his rental car.

"Get in," Brody called out to Braxton as he unlocked the Citroen.

"Who are you?" she asked, buckling into the passenger's seat.

Sliding behind the wheel, Brody said, "My name is Hassan. I work for the Freedom Coalition."

Braxton looked dubious. "You?"

"Yes," Brody said smiling as he pulled away from the curb. "The Germans hire *schwarzes* – and your reaction proves the cover works quite well."

"I need to speak to the man who was with me," Olivia said, her face tightening.

"Relax, Olivia," Brody said. "Ludolph will be fine. I have a partner who'll help him get to safety."

Braxton's face softened after hearing Eltz's name. But she still seemed wary. "How did you know the SS would detain us?"

"The Coalition has been keeping an eye on Ludolph."

"Why?"

"As you've probably gathered, he's something of a novice. But Ludolph's money has bought him friends in high places within the Coalition," Brody said, grateful he'd studied the dossier on Eltz. "I can explain more later, Olivia. Right now, we need to get you out of Francia," he said, turning onto a busy boulevard. "But first, I need to know the status of your op with Ludolph."

Brody knew he was fishing here. There might not be an operation between Eltz and Braxton at all. But he always went with his gut.

"You'll need to ask Ludolph," she answered.

Brody's pulse began to race again. There *was* an op. He had to tread carefully now. "I admire your dedication to security, Olivia. But if my partner fails to find Ludolph, you're our only source. What does the Coalition need to know about your meeting with Ludolph tonight?"

***

I stared at the sky through the windshield, Hassan's question hanging over me. Could I trust him?

I was now an accomplice to murder, to say nothing of the espionage charges from Francia and Virginia. No matter who Hassan worked for, could things get any worse? Then I remembered Dot.

With our op compromised, my comrade in Virginia was now in danger. The charges against Dot for confiscating the C4 would be as severe as my own. But without the phone in my purse, I had no way to warn her. I had to trust Hassan. There was no other choice.

"I need to contact my asset in Virginia – right away," I said. "They need to know I've been burned."

"Of course. You'll have access to a secure line where we're going. You can make the call there," Hassan said. "But it's also important the Coalition know about the status of your op."

"I couldn't get the bloom," I said, still pissed at Eltz for insisting. "But the C4 is on its way."

Hassam was silent for a moment, then nodded. "Thank you. I'll inform the Coalition once you're safe."

"When will we get there?"

"Very soon. I'm taking you to a safehouse here in Paris."

A wave of relief washed over me. I'd rolled the dice. The rest was up to fate.

There was a scrap of pleasure in all this, I realized. I wouldn't have to deal with Eltz again.

Unlike Ludolph, Hassan was a professional. The way he'd duped the SS agents was damned clever. His combat skills were elite, too. Without his help, I'd be facing capital charges.

There was something else I couldn't help noticing. Hassan was easy on the eye. I wasn't sure of his ethnicity. But the guy had gotten head-turning features from at least two different gene pools.

I sank into the car seat and watched the streetlights through the window. The adrenaline from the clash with the SS goons was wearing off. Fatigue was setting in – and a craving for tobacco. "Have anything to smoke?" I asked Hassan. "My vape was in my purse."

Hassan pulled a pack of Admirals from his jacket and shook out a cigarette. "Will this do?"

"How quaint," I said, taking one of the paper-wrapped relics.

"Nicotine is nicotine," he said smiling, then drew an ancient zippo and struck a flame.

I took a long pull from the cigarette. Was this op worth the risks? The question was moot. The life I'd known before was gone.

***

Brody felt a twinge of embarrassment as he led Olivia past a row of sex shops just off Boulevard de Clichy.

Most nations' safehouses were placed in dodgy locations to escape attention. Inside, however, they were usually clean and comfortable. To his chagrin, the interior of Pennsylvania's only safehouse in Paris was of a piece with its seedy neighborhood.

"This way," he said, entering a dark vestibule between the stores. Blocking Olivia's sight from his hands, he tapped the entry code into the keypad hidden under the number plaque on the weathered door. "This is your first stop out of Francia," he said, waving her inside.

They entered the living room of a small apartment. A musty smell rose from the worn couch and chairs clustered around a battered coffee table. An archway behind the living room led to a small kitchen.

"You must be tired," Brody said, then pointed to a door on the right. "That's a bedroom. You can rest there for a while."

Olivia shook her head. "I'd rather call my asset in Virginia."

Brody tried not to smile. Olivia was playing right into his hand. "I'll need a minute to set up the call," Brody said, then walked into the room on the left where he'd been sleeping and closed the door behind him.

Using the encrypted VPN line on his phone, Brody sent a text message to his boss in Philadelphia:

Find out who owns the number of the next call on my phone. They will lead us to Virginia's source of bloom.

***

As soon as Hassan closed the door, I began to pace. The SS would find the dead agents soon. Every minute I waited in reaching Dot could make a difference.

Desperate for a distraction, I walked into the kitchen, looking for a drink.

Opening one of the cupboards, I noticed a hand-written note taped to the inside of the door. Written in English, it was a recipe for scrapple – a favorite meal in Pennsylvania.

My knees weakened for a moment. This place was not German.

Clues to the hoax washed over me in a wave ...Hassan's race ... the old-school cigarettes ...the shabby place ...the scrapple. This had to be the work of the People's Republic of Pennsylvania.

Carrying my heels to soften my footsteps, I ran for the front door.

Rushing outside, I looked around. The street was quiet between the sex shops. Less than twenty paces away was Boulevard de Clichy. Although it was past midnight, the divided street was thick with cars and the sidewalks were full.

Where could I go?

I had no phone, no money, no vehicle and no more than a few minutes lead on the PRP agent who called himself Hassan.

***

With his telephone prepared to snare Olivia's asset in Virginia, Brody opened the bedroom door and walked into the safehouse living room.

"We're ready for your call to..." Brody said before realizing he was alone.

After looking in the other bedroom, Brody walked into the kitchen. There, he saw the open cupboard – and the note taped inside the door.

"Goddammit!" he yelled. He'd never made a meal in this kitchen. Clearly, a previous occupant of the safehouse had – a stupid one.

Brody opened the kitchen door leading into the garage. After pushing the button that opened the garage door, Brody put a fresh clip in his Glock, donned a helmet and leather jacket, and mounted the electric motorbike.

There was still a chance to catch her, he told himself, speeding down the alley. Without a vehicle, a phone or money, Olivia would not get far.

***

Still carrying my heels, I bolted from the safehouse. I ran past the sex shops and headed toward the glow of streetlights and traffic on Boulevard de Clichy.

The sidewalks were clogged with a mix of strolling tourists and trolling professional women. After putting on my heels, I walked to the edge of the curb and scanned the stream of vehicles, looking for a vacant taxi or an eCAB. Getting away fast was all that mattered. I'd figure out how to pay for the ride later.

Instead of a cab, a white Fiat Panda pulled to the curb beside me. Leaning low so I could see him through the window, the driver said, "You up for some CBJ tonight, *bébé?*"

I opened the door and slid into the boxy sedan.

I didn't know what CBJ was. But I sure as hell knew this was a chance to escape.

"How much?" the john asked, putting a hand on my thigh. He wore a gold chain that nestled into the sweaty folds of flesh around his neck.

Fighting a wave of revulsion, I wracked my brain for an answer. He was not going to drive away without a price. "The usual," I finally said.

"You must be new around here," the john said, pulling away from the curb. "I figured a classy babe like you would charge more," he said, still patting my thigh.

I looked down at his hand, wanting to punch him in the face. "Times are hard. You do whatever it takes," I said, trying to buy time. Every minute on the road carried me farther away from the PRP agent who called himself Hassan.

"You talk like a nic. But you don't look like one," he said. "Where are you from?"

"How about we stick to business?"

"Fine by me, *bébé*. Just trying to make some conversation," he said, then turned off Boulevard de Clichy onto a dark side street. "This is a nice quiet spot."

I considered my options as the john pulled to the curb. He turned off the car and killed the headlights beside a row of commercial buildings closed for the night. I was not very far from the PRP safehouse. Getting out here without money or a phone would be pointless.

As the john began to unzip his trousers, I took off my shoe. In an instant, I had the stiletto heel pressed against his neck. "Don't move, motherfucker," I said coldly. "If I press one more centimeter on your carotid artery, you'll bleed to death like a stuck pig."

The john froze. "I don't want any trouble," he said, voice trembling.

"Now, very slowly, take out your wallet and your phone." After the john complied, I said, "Place them on the dashboard and put your hands in your pockets."

Still holding the heel against his neck, I took the wallet and phone, slid them down the front of my dress, then opened the door and stepped out of the car.

The john started the engine and hurried away. "You'll be sorry, *pute!*" he yelled through the window.

***

After reaching Boulevard de Clichy, Brody guided the motorbike alongside the curb near a pair of femmes plying their wares.

"Good evening, ladies," he said, taking off his helmet. "I'm looking for a friend. I think she may be lost."

After describing Olivia, one of the women said, "Tell your 'friend' she's not welcome here. She picked up one of our regulars about ten minutes ago. If she does that again, it's going to go badly for her."

"Which way did they go?"

The woman shrugged. "I don't remember."

"My apologies," Brody said, then opened his wallet and handed her some cash. "It won't happen again,"

She jerked her thumb toward the west. "He drives a white Fiat."

Brody nodded. "Thank you," he said, then put on his helmet and sped down the street.

A block later, his mobile buzzed. Brody pulled into a parking spot and read the text from his boss:

Still waiting to trace that call.

Brody tapped out a reply:

Change of plans. Stand by.

His boss wrote back:

Less than 24 hours left.

"Tell me something I don't know," Brody muttered to himself, merging the motorbike into the flow of traffic.

***

The two constables on foot patrol at a roundabout on Boulevard de Clichy saw a white Fiat screech to a halt beside them. "She stole my wallet! She took my phone!" the driver yelled, getting out of the car.

The police sergeant raised her palm. "Calm down, sir. What's the problem?" she asked as the man walked closer.

"A *pute*, officer," he said, eyes wide. "The crazy bitch put a knife to my neck and threatened to kill me like a pig. Then she made off with my wallet and phone."

"Where did this happen?" the sergeant asked.

"Three streets back, off Boulevard de Clichy," he said, pointing behind the Fiat. "I can take you there in my car."

"That won't be necessary. We can send a mobile unit," she said. "You said she took your phone. I can have it traced if you give me the password."

The john shook his head. "I don't remember it. I always use my thumb."

"Can you give me a description of this woman?"

"Blonde hair. Wearing a black dress and high heels."

"That describes a lot of women around here, no?"

"She didn't look like a regular *pute*. She looked more classy. No cheap jewels or heavy makeup."

"Is there anything else you can tell us about her?"

"She talked like a nic, but she didn't look like one."

The sergeant nodded. "All right. I'll alert our mobile units to look for her," she said, reaching for the two-way radio on her belt.

***

I entered the restroom of a café on a side street off Boulevard de Clichy. After locking myself in a stall, I took stock of my first haul as a mugger. I had a wallet with 2,300 francs and a single credit card. The mobile phone was locked.

The haul was worth shit.

Using the money to hail a cab on Boulevard de Clichy was too risky now. The PRP agent would already be prowling the busy street. The credit card would give away my location the moment I used it. And worst of all, I could not use the locked phone to warn Dot.

For a moment, I thought of using the john's money to buy a burner. Then I remembered: Francia required an ID to buy any phone – and my ID was in my lost purse.

The only choice I had left made my bile rise. I'd need to contact Ludolph Eltz.

The SS agents who tried to arrest me didn't seem to know who Eltz was. So it was unlikely anyone had been sent to detain him. Better still, I had a method to reach Eltz that did not require a phone.

Walking out of the restroom stall, I saw a glint of hope. Our dead drop spot at Parc Poyet was less than three kilometers away. I'd walk there and leave the usual signal. As a precaution, I'd stay away from busy streets. Hassan would be looking for me – and possibly the police. The john might have reported me as a mugger without any fear of the cops. Prostitution was legal in Paris.

With Ludolph's help, I could get word to Dot – and still get safely out of Francia to England. Meantime, Eltz could complete their mission at the Arc de Triomphe.

Returning to the street, I ditched the john's wallet and his phone into a curbside dumpster. At the next corner, I turned toward Parc Poyet along a dark street parallel to the busy Boulevard de Clichy.

Stay calm, I told myself. *You can still get out of this scrape.*

Three blocks into my walk toward the park, I saw a pair of police officers on bicycles cross on a street ahead. One of the officers turned to look at me as they passed.

I stopped and glanced around, looking for a hiding place in case the cops turned back. There were no alleys or alcoves where I could duck out of sight. The smart play now was to keep walking and hope for luck.

When the headlamps of a pair of bicycles appeared at the corner of the block ahead, my heart sank. The cops were coming back.

***

Brody gunned the motorbike until he reached the intersection of the deserted street. There, he stopped and scanned both ways. Not seeing a white Fiat along the cross street, he accelerated to the next intersection.

He'd been repeating this pattern for the last ten minutes. Men paying for sex usually chose dark, deserted side streets like these, not far from where they picked up the women.

Learning that Olivia had accepted an offer from a john had not surprised him. Few diplomats – male or female – would have had the nerve to step into a car with a randy stranger. But Olivia could take care of herself. Brody knew from her dossier that she'd been a soldier – and was feisty as hell based on how she'd battled the SS agent. The john that picked her up was probably in for a surprise.

Arriving at the next intersection, Brody spotted Olivia about a half block away. The sight surprised him.

Facing away from him, she was running down the sidewalk, high heels in hand. Two bicycle cops behind her were pedaling furiously in pursuit. "Halt! Police!" the cops screamed.

Brody turned off the headlamp on the vespa. *Shit*, he thought, driving toward them. *This woman is a toad magnet.*

As he got nearer, Brody could see the cops were about to nab her. One had pedaled ahead and herded her back toward his partner. As he expected, Olivia was putting up a fight. By the time he reached them, the dismounted cops had Olivia pressed against the steel grate over the window of a shuttered tobacco shop. Their sidepieces were holstered as they struggled to handcuff her.

Brody was grateful for the vespa's near-silent engine. In their efforts to restrain Olivia, the cops had not noticed his arrival.

Brody drew his Glock and stepped off the motorbike. "Let her go!" he yelled from a few paces away.

The policemen's eyes widened as they turned and saw a 9mm pistol leveled at them by a man in a leather jacket and motorcycle helmet. When Olivia met his gaze, Brody said, "I'll shoot the first one of you fuckers who moves."

No one moved.

"You," Brody said to the cop on the left, "cuff your partner to the grate."

When that was done, Brody spoke to Olivia. "Take his handcuffs," he said, nodding toward the second cop. "Cuff him to the grate, too."

With both policemen helpless, Brody nodded toward his motorbike and said, "You know how to drive one of these?"

"Yes," Olivia said.

"Put on your shoes and get on," Brody said, keeping the gun trained on her.

Once she mounted the vespa, Brody straddled the bike behind her and pressed the Glock against her ribs. "Drive," he said coldly.

***

The bike cops handcuffed to the pawn shop grate watched helplessly as the madman and his hostage sped away.

"Can you reach my two-way with your foot?" the senior officer asked his partner, nodding toward the radio attached to his belt.

"Good idea," his partner said. Stretching out his leg, the policeman pressed the toe of his shoe against the radio's talk button. "Dispatch, this is Unit 17. Over," he called out.

"Go ahead 17," the dispatcher answered.

"Alert all units in the area. We have a male armed perp with a female hostage. They're on a motorbike heading east on Rue d'Orsel."

***

"Are we going back to your safehouse?" I asked in English after we pulled away from the pawn shop. Although I couldn't see his face, I was certain this was the PRP agent who called himself Hassan.

Hassan ignored the question. "Turn right at the next street," he answered in our native tongue.

As I steered the motorbike through the corner, I tried to stay calm. I was relieved to escape an arrest by the toads. But my fate as a captive of the PRP wouldn't be any better. My only hope was to evade both.

"Should I still call you Hassan?" I asked, hoping to get inside his cover.

"Why not? It'll make things simpler."

"How did you know the SS would arrest me?"

Before he could answer, the two-toned wail of a police siren rose in the distance.

I looked in the rearview mirror and saw a police sedan about three blocks behind, its emergency lights flashing. Hassan noticed the police as well.

"Turn left at the next intersection," he said. "We'll see if they follow us."

I did as he said. I didn't want to get caught any more than Hassan.

After making the turn, I checked the rearview mirror. "They're still behind us."

"OK, you're going to take the next right. Then be ready to turn left quickly."

As I made the turn, I asked, "Where are we going?"

"You'll know soon enough. Now turn left there, between the bushes."

The turn put us on a paved bicycle path winding uphill through a dimly lit park. Looking back, I was surprised to see the police car still following us, its doors almost touching the shrubs lining the three-meter path. "They're still behind us," I said to Hassan.

"I know. Keep the throttle wide open."

After nearly hitting a tree beside the twisting path, I said, "These curves are getting tighter."

"Lean into the turns. We can't slow down."

I looked in the rearview mirror. The police car was getting closer, its siren growing louder. "Even a near-sighted rookie could pick us off if they get any closer."

"They won't shoot. They think you're a hostage," he said. "Now, listen up. We'll be coming to a fork around the next bend. Take the left path."

When we reached the fork, I did as he said.

The new path was steeper and paved with cobblestones. My teeth rattling from the bumpy surface, I glanced at the rearview mirror. The police sedan was now less than two car lengths behind, its headlights engulfing us in a cone of light.

Ahead, I saw the tops of the domes of the Sacré Coeur Basilica. We were nearing the summit of Montmartre, the highest point in Paris.

"The road is going to get wider when we reach the plaza at the top of the hill," Hassan said. "The police will try to pass us and block our path. Stay close to the railing on the right side of the plaza and get ready to brake hard when I tell you."

As we reached the plaza at the top of the hill, the motorbike surged forward, gaining speed on the flat surface. For the first time, I got a glimpse of the entire basilica, its domes and spires bathed in floodlights. The postcard moment was short lived.

The police car turned onto the plaza, tires squealing above the siren.

"Let them get closer and get ready to brake," Hassan said.

As Hassan predicted, the police car overtook us on the left and swerved to block our path. "Brake hard now!" he said.

I squeezed the brake and fought to keep the bike upright as it fishtailed to a stop. "Good work," Hassan said. "Now take us down that stairway," he said pointing toward a one-meter opening in the railing surrounding the plaza.

"What?" I said, looking down a set of steps running a quarter kilometer down the hill.

"You've got this, Olivia. Do it."

I guided the motorbike through the opening in the railing, opened the throttle and leaned back. The bike's handlebars began to quake like a jackhammer. The headlamp beam stuttered over the steps. Hassan helped keep us upright by holding me against the seat.

As we struck each step, I fought to keep the front wheel straight.

An overcorrection would send us tumbling into a pile of broken bones. My arms began to ache, my brow broke into a sweat.

When we finally reached the bottom of the steps, I stopped the bike and looked back. One of the policemen was coming down the steps on foot.

"He'll never catch us. Get us on that street," Hassan said, pointing to a thoroughfare alongside the park.

I cut across a stretch of grass, over the sidewalk, and onto the deserted street.

"Keep driving until we reach Rue Caulaincourt," Hassan said.

Within a block, we were out of sight of the police.

With the immediate threat of arrest gone, we both understood our temporary alliance had ended. I felt the Glock pressed against my ribs again.

But from Hassan's directions, I'd gained a vital piece of knowledge. We were not headed back to his safehouse. That left two unanswered questions. What did Hassan want from me? And when should I make my move to escape?

***

Ludolph looked through the kitchen window of his apartment toward the gate into Parc Poyet. There was no signal from Olivia.

Was she still alive? For the last three hours, the question had burned in Ludolph's mind.

In hindsight, perhaps giving Olivia the number of his burner might have been more efficient than communicating through this intricate signal. But he'd never trusted nics. Their incompetence was legendary.

I had the quick wits to escape, he reminded himself. Once the brawl had begun outside the nightclub, he'd fled deeper into the alley. Hearing two shots, he turned and saw the bodies of the SS agents on the pavement and the *schwarz* helping Olivia to her feet. He did not look back again until he reached his car. Confident the SS agents did not know who he was, Ludolph headed home.

At his apartment, Ludolph brought his Sauer out of the closet, released the safety, and placed the pistol in the top drawer of his desk.

He was safe for now. But if the SS managed to catch Olivia again, she might reveal their plans for the attack – and implicate him. That made her very dangerous.

Olivia had served her purpose. He knew where and when the explosives for their attack on the Arc would arrive from Virginia. The only thing she brought to their mission now was risk.

Adding to the danger she posed was a mystery. Who was the *schwarz* that rescued her?

Only one thing made sense. He would need to eliminate Olivia.

If she left a signal a Parc Poyet, Ludolph would have *Le Fleurist* take care of the problem.

***

Through the window of the wine shop, Brody saw the eCAB arrive. "Our ride is here," he said to Olivia, stubbing out an Admiral.

Brody had led them to this all-night store after ditching the motorbike and helmet at a public parking space a few blocks away. With more than a dozen other two-wheelers parked in the streetside lot, the cops would not find the motorbike anytime soon.

Holding Olivia's arm, Brody looked both ways along the street before leaving the shop. There were no police in sight.

"Where are we going?" she asked as they stepped outside.

"Someplace safe. Please keep quiet," he said, nudging the gun against her side through his jacket. "We're both at risk."

Once they were in the back of the sedan, the driver turned to face them. "Hotel Durant, yes?" he asked, tapping the destination already displayed on his dashboard-mounted phone.

By his accent and complexion, Brody guessed the driver was Haitian. "Yes, thank you," he answered.

"Having some fun tonight?" the driver asked smiling.

Brody looked at Olivia. Her face was grim. "You might say that," he told the driver. "But my date is getting tired. She might appreciate some quiet."

"Sure thing, bruh," the driver said.

Brody looked at Olivia again. Getting her to name those responsible for sending the bloom to Virginia would have been easier at the safehouse. But with the police on high alert for them in the Clichy district, going back there was out.

He'd need to get those names from Olivia soon. He was running out of time before the raid on the Charlottesville armory kickstarted a war.

When they arrived at the hotel, Brody made sure to tip the driver well – but not well enough to make himself memorable.

1801

CHÂTEAU DE FONTAINEBLEAU, FRANCE

Charles-Maurice de Talleyrand paused after entering the richly decorated antechamber. Beyond the ornate door before him was the monarch's private dining salon at Château de Fontainebleau – a place that held a well of memories.

The first time Talleyrand had been summoned to the salon, Louis XVI had been on the throne. After Louis was decapitated during the revolution, Talleyrand had met there with Robespierre and the Committee of Public Safety. Now, Talleyrand was returning from England as the foreign minister for the new emperor of France. Few other men had ever served the procession of occupants at Fontainebleau – and kept their heads.

Talleyrand opened the door and walked inside. At the head of the table was Napoleon Bonaparte with the empress Josefine on his right.

"Your Majesty, I bring news from England," Talleyrand said, holding out his document case.

The emperor waved toward one of the chairs. "Sit, Talleyrand. We were about to eat – but that can wait."

"I hope you bring us good news, Talleyrand," Josefine said. "My husband has been insufferable. He's done little but worry about this treaty since you left."

Weighing his reply as he took a chair, the prime minister said, "Madame, a gracious head of state should constantly fret for the wellbeing of his subjects, no?"

Napoleon raised his palm. "Let's dispense with concerns about my temperament – and the flattery," he said. "Did George accept our terms?"

Talleyrand had been sent by Napoleon to negotiate a peace treaty with England's George III. Napoleon's victory at Waterloo had decimated Wellington's army and left England at risk of an invasion.

"Almost all your terms were met, Your Majesty," Talleyrand said, then took France's copy of the treaty out of the case and placed it on the table.

Napoleon stood, leaned over the lengthy document and scowled. "What did George refuse?"

"I added a clause that King George should polish your boots every morning," the minister said smiling. "On that, he was implacable."

Slapping the table, Napoleon burst into laughter. "You're a sly one, Talleyrand. I sent the right man to England."

Conveyed through Talleyrand, Napoleon's demands from England were punishing. But with his island virtually defenseless, a dejected King George had agreed. England would vacate her naval bases in Gibraltar, Halifax and Jamaica. Most importantly,

George would cede all remaining English territory in
North America to France."

I'm honored by your approval, Sire," Talleyrand
said. "But there are still some thorns among the roses
that I bring you."

"What are these thorns, Talleyrand?" Josefine
asked the foreign minister.

Napoleon answered instead. "England's former
colonies in North America."

"As always, Your Majesty is a step ahead,"
Talleyrand said. "Yes, these shabby countries are
independent from England and will impede our
dominion over the continent," he said. "We should
prepare for their conquest as soon as possible."

"Why do men always think war is the answer to
every problem?" Josefine asked.

Talleyrand placed a hand on his chest. "With all
due respect, My Lady, how else would we remove
these impediments to our destiny?"

"Make them our vassals," Josefine said. "If they're
as poor as you say, that should not be difficult."

Napoleon rubbed his chin. "I think the empress
makes a fair point. Why not profit from these devils
instead of draining the treasury to raise another
army."

"The expense would not be great, Sire," Talleyrand
said. "We can rout them with a few divisions."

Shaking his head, Napoleon said, "The English
no doubt shared your opinion of these Britannics,
Talleyrand. But they fought fiercely and won their
independence."

"You've proven our superiority to the English on
the battlefield, Sire." Talleyrand said. "Your victory
at Waterloo has already brought Austria, Germany
and Poland under our control. Surely, we can defeat a

gaggle of English outcasts."

"If we send our troops across the ocean, we weaken ourselves in Europe. I agree with the empress. Why risk a distant war if we can profit from peace?"

"You explained the importance of North America before I left for England, Sire," Talleyrand said. "Have you changed your mind?"

"Not in the least," the emperor said. "I still believe finding the northwest passage to the orient will bring great wealth to our empire. But we can develop that route through Quebec and New Orleans. We don't need the Britannic seaports."

"Still, these nations pose a risk to our trade routes."

"If one of these paltry little countries dares to take up piracy against us, then it will know my true wrath."

Talleyrand lowered his head. "As you wish, Your Majesty."

"There is one other thing, Talleyrand. Thanks to this treaty, our territory now extends far beyond Europe. France is no longer bound by its ancient borders. Therefore, I will soon proclaim that our global empire be called Francia."

~=~

1802

RALEIGH, NORTH CAROLINA

In the only chair of a meager boardinghouse room, Thomas Jefferson scoured the *North Carolina Examiner* for news from Virginia. Finding only reports of ship arrivals and departures from the port of Norfolk, he put down the newspaper and stared out the window.

His life had come undone with mind-numbing swiftness.

Two years ago, he'd taken pride in walking to his inauguration without a security detail, accompanied only by a few friends. He believed a president should have the trust of his people. Not long after taking office as Virginia's head of state, Jefferson regretted overestimating the honor of his landsmen – and his popularity among them.

He should have kept a unit of guards nearby as his chief of staff had advised – and had an evacuation plan.

When a breathless aide arrived with news
that Washington's troops were marching on the
presidential residence, Jefferson's only recourse had
been to gather his daughters and their families and
flee. He could not abide the disgrace of becoming a
captive.

Rumors of a move against him by Washington had
been swirling for weeks. Jefferson had brushed them
aside. He refused to believe his rival would ever resort
to a coup d'état. But like Caesar, Washington had
crossed the Rubicon and betrayed his nation.

Despite his treachery, Washington still had many
supporters. Jefferson could not deny that.

During Jefferson's first year as Virginia's president,
he'd resurrected his dream of unity among the former
colonies. The time had come. He now had the power
to influence his countrymen.

His proposal for a third Continental Congress had
been dead-on-arrival at the House of Delegates.

Meanwhile, the economy plummeted. The political
upheaval in France that brought Napoleon to power
slashed demand for tobacco from Virginia. The
plantation owners blamed Jefferson, even though
the problem was beyond his control. The faltering
economy became fodder for the reprisal of old
scandals.

He was again pilloried for Pennsylvania's
annexation of Maryland and Delaware. And, of
course, the ugly editorials about his life with Sally
Hemings surfaced in the press for a second time. Ever
the pettifogger, Washington had made sure these old
disgraces found new life.

All that had been a prelude to the greatest blow of
all.

When Pennsylvania occupied New Jersey, a frenzy

of recrimination engulfed Virginia.

Not surprisingly, after Washington took the presidency by force, public outcry was muted. Even those in Jefferson's own party laid low, fearing they would fall victim to the upheaval as well.

That was three months ago.

Jefferson was now an exile in North Carolina, living apart from his daughters and using an assumed name, Robert Harwell. Washington had spies everywhere and there were many who wanted him dead. His daughters Martha and Maria, along with their husbands and children, were safer being away from him. He'd sent them to stay with friends in Georgia.

Jefferson chose to remain close to Virginia – despite the risks.

Washington would inevitably stumble. He always had, the oaf. When the opportunity came, Jefferson wanted to be nearby and ready to reclaim the presidency he had legitimately earned.

In the meantime, Jefferson had taken up residence in a Raleigh boardinghouse posing as an itinerant surveyor – a skill he hoped to ply soon. The money he'd managed to leave with from Virginia was almost gone.

Sitting in this cramped room at the boarding house, his days in Monticello and Richmond now seemed like another life. The memory of those times reminded Jefferson how easily one grew complacent with the privileges of wealth – until they were gone.

Looking for hopeful news abroad, Jefferson returned to the newspaper. What he found was devastating.

Napoleon had signed a peace treaty with a war-weary England. George III had granted Napoleon control over all the English territory in North America. Before long, the Britannic nations would be completely surrounded by the most powerful empire on earth. Bonaparte had named it Francia.

Jefferson had hoped to see a union of states that spanned a continent, a place where independent thinkers could fulfill their destinies, where the bold would be rewarded. Napoleon had cornered the former British colonies and crushed that hope.

Their destiny now seemed clear. Virginia, and all its English-speaking neighbors, would become petty fiefdoms mired in turmoil and poverty, forever under Francia's thumb.

Two knocks on the door were followed by the voice of his housemistress from the hallway. "Supper is ready, Mister Harwell," she called out as the aroma of stew rose from the kitchen.

"Thank you, Mrs. Landry," he answered. "I'll not be eating this evening."

For a while now he'd been contemplating another letter to his daughters Martha and Maria – the last one. Lighting a candle against the fading sunlight, Jefferson took quill in hand and began to write.

My dearest daughters,

Despite the tragic loss of your mother, I had the good fortune to raise you at Monticello, a place where you never had want or need. Through my own failings, you no longer enjoy these blessings which you so richly deserve. The duty of a father takes many forms. I regret all the ways in which I've failed you as provider and protector.

There comes a time when a man must face his

shortcomings. That time has come for me. I cannot see a way to redeem myself, nor ever regain what I have lost.

The only legacy I have left to bequeath you is one of honor. Yet, even in this, my decision will bring you pain. Though you are both innocent, you will once again bear the brunt of my failures. To help me atone, I ask that you keep my promises to those serving our household back home.

I hope you'll forgive me. 'Tis not for lack of affection for you that I've come up short.

Your forever loving father

He tucked the letter into an envelope, addressed it to his daughters, and placed it on the center of the room's small desk. Slipping a flintlock into his coat, Jefferson walked outside.

There was a small glen not far away. He'd finish this business there.

MONTICELLO, VIRGINIA

Thomas Jefferson's body was buried near his former plantation in Virginia six days later. Within the month, his daughters and their families, along with a few close relations, gathered for a private memorial service.

President Washington, in a gesture of respect for his Tidewater neighbor, had given his consent to the proceedings. Privately, Washington believed that neither Jefferson's memory nor the few mourners at his memorial posed any threat. Jefferson was still widely disparaged.

Despite the president's permission, church bells did not toll that day and the service was denied any military pomp. At Jefferson's grave marker, the rector of the local Episcopal church began his eulogy with less than two dozen mourners gathered around him.

In a group closest to the clergyman were Jefferson's daughters Martha and Maria along with their spouses and children. A handful of other relatives stood beside them.

Sally Hemings and her four children stood at a distance behind Jefferson's white mourners. Unlike Martha and Maria's families, who had fled to Georgia, Sally and her family were property of the plantation and had remained in Monticello.

The minister spoke of Thomas Jefferson in words carefully chosen to avoid offending the current president.

"The dreams of our dearly departed were not small. He imagined all the English-speaking nations of America as one indivisible union," the rector said somberly. "That was not to pass. This was not the fate of our beloved Virginia."

As the minister continued, Sally glanced toward her own children. Beverly, Eston, Harriet and Madison had been fathered by Master Tom. They shared as much blood with Thomas Jefferson as Martha and Maria. Yet, her children would forever stand behind their lily-white half-sisters.

After the rector finished his eulogy and the final prayer was said, Martha, Maria and their families walked back toward the big house, never once glancing at Sally and her children – except for one well-built young man Sally did not recognize.

The young man approached Sally and nodded. "My name is Aaron Braxton. I'm Martha and Maria's cousin, on their mother's side."

"I appreciate your courtesy, Mr. Braxton," Sally said, lowering her eyes.

"My cousin Martha sent me with some good news, ma'am," he said. "Her husband has drawn up manumission documents for you and your children. Once they're signed, all of you will be free."

Sally closed her eyes as they welled with tears. The man she'd called Thomas in private had kept his word. For that much, she was grateful. But she had no illusions about their relationship.

She'd been fourteen and a handmaid for Maria when the widowed master took an interest in her. Sally soon learned his kind words and small gifts came with a price. Over time, she learned to bargain with Thomas. After bearing him four children, the last bargain had been their freedom.

But the news Braxton brought made Sally uneasy. "Why didn't Miss Martha tell me herself?" Sally had helped raise Martha and her sister after their mother died.

Braxton lowered his gaze. "Martha feels people may spread more rumors about her father if this involves her directly. As you know, his memory is under a cloud at present."

Sally nodded. "I see," she said, staring at the ground.

Thomas had been no different than most masters. The sight of all the light-skinned folks in the slave quarters of any plantation in Virginia was proof enough of that. But the secrets at Monticello went deeper.

Sally's father had been a slave owner named John

Wayles, the man whose white wife had given birth to Martha Wayles – Thomas' wife who'd died in childbirth. In truth, Sally was the aunt of Thomas' white daughters.

But in the eyes of most Tidewater families, this had not been Thomas' greatest sin. His sin had been doing too little to hide the truth.

Braxton touched Sally's sleeve, breaking her trance. "May I be introduced to your children?" he asked.

Sally's eyes widened. "Yes, sir. Of course."

After she'd named her offspring, Braxton said, "Thank you, ma'am. I pray the day will come when the world recognizes their connection to my uncle."

"As do I, sir," Sally said. "As do I."

~=~

PARIS, FRANCIA

The eCAB stopped on a narrow, dimly lit street lined with unkept Hausmann buildings. With Hassan gripping my arm, we got out of the car and walked through a door with "Hotel Durant" carved into the worn stone lintel.

During the ride to the hotel, I'd worked out my escape from Hassan. I'd play nice until he let down his guard, then I'd make my move. But I needed to choose that moment wisely. Hassan was a formidable opponent.

"Good evening, sir," the hotel clerk said to Hassan as we approached the front desk. "Glad you're back again."

I said nothing as Hassan had instructed. Knowing a Glock was trained on me through his jacket pocket was a persuasive argument.

After Hassan checked us in, we entered a small, ancient elevator.

Once the elevator door closed, I said, "I take it this hotel is where you bring your *putes*."

Hassan smiled. "That would certainly put you in good company," he said, pushing the button for the third floor.

"Is it wise to hide out in a hotel where you're known?"

"I prefer a place where I know all the exits," he said as we arrived on the third floor.

Walking through the door marked 302, I was relieved to find the room was stylish and well-appointed. Across from a double bed with a large amenity kit on the nightstand was a plasma screen and a mini-bar. A single window had a view of a similar Haussmann building less than ten meters across the narrow street.

"Sit down," Hassan said gesturing toward the room's lone chair near the window.

"I'd rather stand."

Hassan tapped the gun in his pocket, then nodded toward the chair. "I wasn't being polite."

I sat down.

Keeping enough space between us to draw his Glock, Hassan sat down on the bed, his back against the headboard. "OK, by now you've figured out I work for the PRP. Do you still want to contact your asset in Virginia?"

"Yes."

Hassan pulled the phone from his pocket and held it up. "I can make that happen, but we need to make a deal."

"I'm listening."

"Who in the government of Francia authorized the deployment of *munitions biologique* to Virginia?"

"I don't know what you're talking about."

"Playing dumb doesn't suit you, Olivia," he said. "You tried to supply the Germans with bloom. Who in Virginia is responsible for that?"

"I'm not going to give up my asset so you can have them killed."

"What good would that do Pennsylvania?" he said, scowling. "The bloom is coming from Francia. If we kill your asset, the toads will just find another virgie stooge to test their weapons."

His insult to Dot went too far. "Fuck you, nic."

Hassan smirked. "I may look black. But the toads don't give a shit that your skin is white. To them, you're still an ignorant nic ... just like me."

I balled my fists and rose to my feet.

Tapping the weapon in his pocket, Hassan said, "Are you going to put your asset in Virginia at risk just to soothe your pride?"

I sat down. I'd need to stay frosty to save Dot – and myself.

"How about we start again?" he said softly.

"I'm still listening."

"Olivia, Francia is my country's enemy. Whatever it is you're planning with the Germans is clearly an op against the toads. So, you and I have a common enemy. We may not be allies, but can we at least call a truce?"

"What are your terms for this truce?"

"Let's lay out our cards. I'll tell you my mission. You tell me yours."

"All right. You go first."

"Pennsylvania can't stop the flow of bloom to North America. Only the toads can. My job is to prove there's a secret pipeline of *munitions biologique* from Francia to Virginia. Once we expose those involved to the media, the opposition party in Francia will force the prime minister to shut down the bloom pipeline. We don't have to kill anyone. Political pressure will do the job."

"You expect me to believe that?"

"I didn't believe it either when my boss first told me. But the more I thought about it, the more it made sense. People like us blow shit up to solve problems, Olivia. But using your enemy's weaknesses against them can be more effective sometimes."

I had to admit his method made sense. My battle with Hassan was the same. I was using guile to thwart a more powerful enemy as well. "It might work," I finally said.

"I've told you my mission. Now, it's your turn."

I took a deep breath. Trusting a PRP agent did not come easily. "I'm providing the Freedom Coalition with ordnance to use against a target in Francia. That attack will launch their war of independence."

"Why would Virginia help the Germans? The toads are your allies."

"No one in Richmond knows anything about this. It's a freelance op by a small group of dissidents in Virginia."

"I have no reason to interfere with your op, Olivia. You and the Germans can blow up as much of Francia as you want," he said. "Hell, I'll help you – if you'll help me find out who in the government of Francia is responsible for providing the bloom to Virginia."

He had a point. Dot might know the people Hassan wanted to find. Exposing those toad motherfuckers could deliver a parting blow before Dot went into hiding. "I'd need to call my asset in Virginia to get those names."

"And you want to warn your asset that you've been burned. Seems we have a win-win,"

Hassan's kumbaya spiel made sense – except for one thing. I'd be dead once Hassan had the names he wanted. I already knew too much for him to let me walk away. "I have another condition to our truce," I said.

Hassan smiled. "I'm listening."

"I want to go to Parc Poyet – now."

***

"Why Parc Poyet?" Brody asked. The demand made no sense – unless she was luring him into a trap.

"That's my business," Olivia answered. "I'll call my asset in Virginia after you've taken me there."

"Why not call now?" he said, holding up the phone. "The longer you wait, the greater the danger. The SS will eventually track down your asset."

"It's a risk I'm willing to take."

Brody knew Olivia was up to something. But time was running out. He'd need to play along – and be very careful. "What's your shoe size?" he asked.

Olivia looked puzzled. "Seven," she said. "Why do you need to know?"

"If we're going out again tonight, we'll need different clothes," he said, dialing his mobile. "Our descriptions are on every gendarme's radio in the city by now."

"You're calling a store at this hour?"

"Better than that," he said as Eva's line rang. When Eva answered, he said, "Good evening, *ma chérie*. Are you free at the moment?"

"I can cancel my next appointment," Eva said.

"That's very sweet. I need a favor."

"Favor? You said the next time would be a real date."

"I'm sorry. Can I make it up by doubling your rate again?"

"You always make life easy, *mon cœur*. What's the favor?"

"I need a set of outdoor clothes for me and a woman about your size. She'll need size seven shoes and a hat as well. Anything you can get your hands on quickly will be fine. Time is more important than fit."

"I can manage that," Eva said. "Where do we meet?"

"Hotel Durant, room 302."

"Ah, yes," she said. "I'll be there shortly."

"*Merci beaucoup, ma chérie*," he said before ending the call.

"You have a personal concierge?" Olivia asked.

"Something like that," Brody said, lighting up two Admirals. He then placed a lit cigarette on an ashtray on the nightstand between them. "Help yourself," he said, stepping back a safe distance.

"Thanks," Olivia said, retrieving the cigarette.

They both smoked in silence for a time, savoring the sensation, their bodies regaining a normal chemistry with a fresh infusion of nicotine.

After stubbing out the last of his Admiral, Brody pointed toward a video screen above the dresser. "You can watch some television while we wait for the clothes."

Olivia's face puckered. "I can't stand the pretentious shit on the tube here. Every other show is an ass-kissing documentary about Napoleon or one of his descendants," she said, then took a long drag on her cigarette. "I like the perks of living in Francia, but I sure as hell miss stock car races."

"Same with me," Brody said. "Not the stock car races. But living in the belly of the beast has its advantages."

"I'm surprised you'll admit that. I thought the party line in the People's Republic is that you live in a workers' paradise."

"I'm not blind, Olivia. I know my government hasn't always lived up to its ideals."

"Lived up to its ideals?" she said with a sneer. "Your country is a nanny state with a bloated, self-serving government full of crooked bureaucrats. Your people live in hovels, your schools are hell holes, and your healthcare is a cruel joke. Without the Soviets, you'd all starve."

Brody's face hardened. "And you live in that glorious bastion of small-government, Virginia," he said. "*Your* idea of a republic is to elect a sham congress of corrupt cronies on the take from toad corporations who help the rich get richer and keep the poor living like peasants."

"The people of Virginia may be poor, but they're free. They're not smothered by socialist overlords who control people's lives in the name of equality."

"In other words, your government does nothing to stop the rich from exploiting the poor."

Olivia rolled her eyes. "That's the kind of small-minded bullshit that's almost brought us to a war again."

"You think it's small minded to respect international boundaries?"

"Our nations agreed in the Treaty of 1866 that our border would be defined by the northernmost tributary of the Potomac. So, if the course of that tributary changes over time, the border changes with it."

"Wrong," Brody said, jabbing his finger. "There's nothing in the treaty about the river changing course."

"That was an oversight in the drafting of the treaty. "What they intended—"

A knock on the door ended their argument.

***

Hassan's scowl faded. "That will be our clothes," he said, "We'll need to continue this conversation another time."

Keeping a wary gaze on me, Hassan walked to the door and opened it.

A woman in a man's trench coat and black high-heeled boots entered the room. Her red hair was cut in a chic bob set off by large loop earrings. "Working late again, I see," she said to Hassan, then placed a plastic bag with clothes on the bed. As she removed the garments from the bag, her trench coat opened, revealing a black bustier.

"Thank you for bringing these, *ma chérie*," Hassan said, rummaging through the clothes. "Did you bring shoes?"

From the bottom of the bag, the woman pulled a pair of bright pink trainers with gold leaf trim. "I wear them for my aerobics class. They're all I could find at this hour."

I tried not to shudder. The thought of wearing those ridiculous shoes made me cringe.

The redhead noticed my reaction. "A little too much style for you, princess?" she asked with a sour look.

Hassan tossed the shoes across the room to me. "Try them on."

I pulled on the gym shoes and laced them up. "They're too small," I said grimacing.

"I'm sorry. They'll have to do," Hassan said. "We're running out of time."

"I found this for *you*," the redhead said, handing Hassan a blue sports jersey with a yellow 17 across the chest. "You'll look like another crazy Lyon fan."

As Hassan took off his shirt and pulled on the jersey, I couldn't help noticing his sculpted torso. "Who is number seventeen?" I asked.

"You don't know Marco?" the redhead said to me. She then looked at Hassan. "What dungeon have you been keeping *her* in?"

Hassan smiled. "My friend is not a fan of Bataille."

"Ah," the redhead said, rumpling her nose. "Another Britannic. I should have known."

I sneered at her. "It's amusing to see how little it takes to make a whore feel superior."

"I'll slap that smile right off your face, *garce*," the redhead said.

Hassan stepped between us and took out his wallet. "Thank you, *ma chérie*," he said, handing the redhead a wad of francs. "You're a lifesaver, as always."

"Take care of yourself, *mon cœur*," the redhead said, putting the money into her pocket. "I think you've got a viper on your hands."

After the redhead was gone, Hassan put all the women's clothes back in the bag and tossed it to me. "You can go in the bathroom to change clothes. But keep the door open. I don't want you getting any ideas about the window in there."

This was a chance to show Hassan he didn't intimidate me.

I pulled the thin straps off my shoulders and stepped out of the black dress. Standing in my skivvies, I said, "I've changed clothes in front of men before in the army. Women wear less at the beach." Then I reached for the clothes the redhead had brought. After pulling a pair of baggy sweatpants over my shoes, I put on a t-shirt, parka and a baseball cap.

While I was changing clothes, I watched Hassan swap his black leather jacket for a light-blue windbreaker and put his Glock in a pocket. Hassan then retrieved the mobile from his leather jacket. "I'll get us an eCAB to Parc Poyet," he said, dialing the phone.

"Have the driver take us to the convenience store near the south entrance to the park," I said, pulling my hair into a ponytail through the back of the cap. "I'll explain why when we get there."

***

The eCAB drove away, leaving them in a patch of light on the sidewalk from the RapideMart storefront. Across the street, cloaked in darkness, was the south entrance to Parc Poyet.

"What now?" Brody asked Olivia.

"Follow me," she said, crossing the desolate street.

Entering the park, Olivia led them along a winding footpath, barely visible in the glow of the streetlights surrounding the unlit greenspace. The shapes of trees and shrubs created patches of black along their route. Despite the dim light, Brody noticed the park was unkempt. Broken branches and piles of leaves cluttered the walkway.

Suddenly wary, Brody blocked her path and drew his pistol.

"I'm not sure where you're taking me, Olivia. Please don't make me do anything that violates our truce."

"Keep your gun on me if that makes you feel better," she said, walking around him. "Come on. We're almost there."

As they neared the streetlights on the north side of the park, Olivia stopped. "I need to find two stones about the size of a lemon," she said, scanning the ground alongside the path.

Once she'd found the rocks, Olivia said, "Stay here," and began walking.

Brody grabbed her arm. "Where are you going?"

"I'm going to place these rocks by that lamppost," she said, pointing toward the streetlight at the north entrance to the park.

"I'll go with you," Brody said.

"You can't," she said. "If you're seen with me, this won't work."

"What won't work?"

Olivia's face grew stern. "All right, Hassan. Here's what's going to happen," she said. "The stones are a signal that will bring Ludolph Eltz to this park. Once Eltz is here, I'll call my asset on your phone and let them know I've been burned. I'll also ask my asset for the names you want," she said. "But I need to be sure you don't kill Eltz and me once you have those names," she said. "So you're going to let me leave with Eltz. Once I'm safe, I'll call you with the names," she said, then added, "This is not negotiable."

"Why should I believe you'll call me with the names?"

"Why should I believe you won't kill me once you have them?" she countered. "I'd say we're at an impasse."

Olivia's savvy impressed Brody. Although he had the upper hand, she'd forced him into a draw. But there was one flaw in her plan. "Can you trust Eltz?" he asked.

"Why not?"

"You said he already knows the time and place your C4 will arrive?"

"That's right."

"Then why does Eltz need *you*?"

Olivia blinked. "He's an ally. You're an enemy," she finally said.

"Yes. But we have a truce, remember?"

"Good. I'll be back," she said, then started walking out of the shadows toward the streetlights, stones in hand. Over her shoulder, she said, "Keep your gun trained on me if you want. Just stay out of sight."

Brody put away his Glock. To get those names, he'd have to trust Olivia.

***

Ludolph parted the curtains of his kitchen window.

"I have her now," he said to himself, a smile spreading on his face.

There, by the ornate steel light post at the entrance to Parc Poyet, were two stones.

For more times than he could remember that night, he'd checked for Olivia's signal. He'd tried taking short naps, setting a timer on his phone. But his anxiety – and four cups of Turkish coffee – had kept him awake.

Ludolph turned and scanned the kitchen, looking for his phone. Wandering into the living room, he grabbed the burner from an end table next to the sofa where he'd tried fruitlessly to sleep. The number he wanted was already on his list of recent calls.

"Your target has left a message at the designated location in Parc Poyet," Ludolph said when *Le Fleurist* answered. "Meet with her wherever her note says, then call me when the job is done."

"Copy," *Le Fleurist* said and ended the call.

A smile of relief spread across Ludolph's face. It was a shame he could not celebrate this moment with his wife. She was spending the night at her lover's apartment.

***

I led Hassan to the recycling bin in the park where Eltz would come for the message. "We need to hide," I said. "Ludolph might get spooked and leave if he sees anyone around."

"That's not surprising," Hassan said as they left the footpath and walked into the deep shadows under a cluster of trees. "He bolted like a rabbit at *Le Velours Bleu.*"

"Ludolph is paranoid. He's the one who insisted on the dead drop. It's just silly cloak and dagger shit."

Hassan looked at his watch. "We might be here until morning," he said. "Eltz may be at home asleep by now."

I shook my head. "He lives near here, within sight of the entrance. I'm sure of that," I said. "And, trust me, he'll be up all-night checking for the stones. The signal will assure him I haven't been arrested and he's out of danger, too."

Hassan cleared the grass of several large dead limbs between a pair of trees and then sat down. "We might as well get comfortable."

Joining him on the ground, I took off my shoes. "These silly fucking things are killing my feet," I said, rubbing my instep.

Although the light was dim, Olivia saw Hassan smile. "I'm sorry," he said. "But you have to admit, they're an improvement over the heels."

"Thank you, Captain Obvious," I said. "I'll make it a point to leave the spike heels at home on my next combat op."

"I know you were in the military. Isn't that rare for a woman in your country?"

"You can stop the soft interrogation, Hassan."

"Honestly, I'm just trying to make conversation," he said. "I sure as hell don't want to get us back on politics."

"Probably a good idea."

"Can we talk about the weather?"

"That's usually a safe topic," I said, putting on the pink and gold shoes again.

"They say springtime in Paris is romantic," he said, buttoning the collar of his windbreaker. "I think it's kind of clammy."

"No hurricanes, though," I said. "Each year, they seem to get worse back home."

"Yeah, that's true up our way, too."

"The countryside around Paris reminds me of home," I said. "A lot of the trees are the same as Virginia's."

"Yeah. It's a shame these gits all speak French, though. Sorta ruins the place."

I laughed. For the first time since *Le Velours Bleu*, the knot in my stomach relaxed. "Wow. I think we just had a normal moment."

"Yeah," he said, then looked away.

Uncomfortable with the sudden intimacy, we both fell into silence.

Until this moment, I'd seen Hassan only as an enemy. Now, we had crossed a hazy line. He was in many ways like me. We both spoke the same language. Our ancestors had lived near the same mountains, fished on the same ocean. We were more alike than—

From the corner of my eye, I saw something moving and rose to my feet.

"Someone's coming," I said, pointing toward the footpath. Although the figure was a dark shape backlit by the streetlights,

I knew this was not Ludolph. Instead of Eltz's short, dumpy frame, the man walking toward us was someone powerfully built and large. Very large.

The contrast did not escape Hassan. "That's not Eltz," he said, standing up.

"Maybe Ludolph sent someone to get the message. He's not one for heroics."

"That's possible," Hassan said. "Or he may have sent a mechanic."

"There's only one way to find out," I said, then started toward the dead drop.

Hassan pulled me back into the shadows. "Stay here," he said. "I'll handle this."

"Sure, so you can kill him and say it was a hitman."

"Fine. Come with me," he said. "But I'll talk to him. Keep quiet – and stay out of the way."

***

Bernard Vannier entered Parc Poyet at a brisk clip. *Le Fleurist* had good reason to hurry. This contract for Eltz would be more difficult to complete in daylight. Besides, he had more important things to do.

He had an audition at eleven in the morning and still needed time to memorize his lines. The part was small, but juicy. And the director had a reputation as a stickler for punctuality.

Walking along the footpath through the trees, Bernard cursed his luck again. Eltz had given him a two-step job: pick up the message with the location, then complete the contract. What if this woman wanted to meet on the other side of the city? This could turn into a disaster.

When Bernard saw the recycling container, he picked up the

pace. The pay for these gigs as a mechanic was good, he reminded himself. He lived much better than most aspiring actors. In fact, he enjoyed playing the tough-talking hitman, *Le Fleurist*. It was good practice for the kind of roles a man his size could get – especially the weapons training. His self-defense classes and gym sessions helped keep him fit, too. A lot of action-adventure superstars had started with less.

Sometimes he felt squeamish about ending the life of a crooked business partner or a cheating wife. But they usually deserved it. Whatever this woman tonight had done, he didn't have time to care.

Arriving at the dead drop spot, Bernard walked behind the recycling container, dropped to one knee, and reached under the bin.

Behind him, he heard an automatic pistol being raked. "You're not going to find a message there," a man's voice said. "Now, stand up. Very slowly."

Bernard rose to his feet. He knew turning around would be foolish. Whoever this was did not want to be seen – and he knew about his contract. "What do you want?"

"Ludolph Eltz sent me. I'm his insurance policy."

"What does that mean?"

"Your target is a woman. Eltz wants to be sure you're up to the job."

"I've done women before. That's not a problem."

"I'm glad to hear that," the voice said. "Now get on your knees."

Bernard's heart began to pound. Something had gone wrong. This man might have been sent to kill *him*.

Without looking, he launched a kick toward the voice.

***

The big man's boot struck Brody in the sternum, sending him to the ground.

Gasping for breath, his Glock out of reach, Brody saw the giant looking down at him. As the man reached into his jacket for a weapon, Olivia stepped out of the shadows behind the hitman and swung a thick tree branch into the back of his head.

The giant staggered for a moment and Olivia struck again. Like a felled tree, he collapsed.

Propping himself on an elbow, Brody watched as Olivia dropped the tree branch and picked up his gun.

"Unlock your phone and give it to me," she said pointing the Glock at him.

Breathing hard from the pain, Brody said. "Put down the gun, Olivia. Eltz wants you dead. You're not going to kill me. I'm the only lifeline you've got left."

"I'll take you with me," she said, her voice cold. "Now unlock that phone."

"I thought we had a truce?"

"The conditions have changed," she said. "I have the gun now."

"That's true," Brody said, rising slowly to his feet. "But there's one thing that hasn't changed. You need me as much as I need you – no matter who's holding the gun. We're going to have to trust each other, Olivia," he said, looking into her eyes. "Either we keep our truce, or you can kill me now."

After a long moment, Olivia lowered the Glock. "We'll keep the truce," she said, then pointed toward the hitman's body. "Take his gun. We may need another one."

Brody removed the weapon from the big man's jacket and tucked it into his own. He then touched the assassin's neck. "He's alive."

"What do you want to do about him?"

"Nothing. We may need the ammo," Brody said. In truth, he found killing repugnant. He regretted dispatching the SS men. Another death was unnecessary.

"You were right about Ludolph," she said, putting the Glock in her parka.

Brody managed a smile. "It was a self-serving guess."

"We need to find a safe place where I can call my asset."

In pain and moving slowly, Brody started down the footpath. "Let's go back to the convenience store. I'll hail an eCAB there and get us back to the hotel."

The hitman's kick might have broken a rib. But that wasn't the worst of it. Two new developments were putting Brody's mission at risk. His leverage over Olivia was gone. And, more dangerous still, Brody's admiration for his feisty adversary was growing.

1818

RICHMOND, VIRGINIA

The cook carried a pitcher of coffee to the large table in the kitchen where the servants at Andrei Durfort's mansion took their meals.

"When do you figure Mademoiselle Claudia will get here?" Emma asked the butler as she filled his cup. The household's highest servants were alone in the large room. The rest of the staff were busy with their duties.

"We've got time to get ready. Monsieur said the day after tomorrow at the earliest," Warren answered before sipping some coffee.

Emma took a chair next to the butler. "I've never seen Monsieur so worked up, Warren. He's like a coon hound with a possum up a tree."

"It's not every day your bride-to-be arrives from Paris."

"You think a fancy lady from Paris is going to like

it here?" she asked, pouring coffee into her cup.

"Monsieur met her on his last trip to Francia. My understanding is that Mademoiselle is not an aristocrat like Monsieur."

"Just because she's not fancy doesn't mean she's going to take to Virginia."

"Well, I'm going to make sure the entire staff does their best to welcome her – and that includes you, Emma."

"Yes, sir. Mister Butler, sir," she said with an exaggerated bow.

From the long row of bells hanging on the wall, the one from the study rang.

Warren put down his cup and stood. "I'll see what Monsieur needs."

"You tell him I said he needs to calm himself down, you hear?"

The butler rolled his eyes and left.

Emma knew that Monsieur's love of her cooking gave her license to joke in ways that would have had another servant flogged.

She thanked the Lord for having a master from Francia. Virginia masters were harsh – when they weren't trying to get under your skirts. Maybe slavery being illegal in Francia had something to do with that. In any case, Monsieur was an honest-to-God gentleman and had never laid a finger on her. For any reason.

That's not to say Monsieur was a saint. There was talk he made his fortune in Virginia with some sharp dealing. They said he'd put a lot of Virginia tobacco agents out of business when he came to Richmond because he was rich enough to undercut their commissions. But what difference did that make to her? White folks' idea of being poor was eating with pewter forks.

Well, not all white folks. Warren wasn't from a Tidewater family. All the same, he'd gone to school and eventually become a teacher at William and Mary. But with four children, Warren found being a butler for a rich Frank paid better. Emma knew Warren was glad to have the job, too. A lot of white men wanted it. That Warren could speak French had clinched it.

Warren entered the kitchen, his face flushed. "Plans have changed. Mademoiselle is arriving tomorrow. We need to start getting dinner ready right away."

"Tomorrow?" As the cook at the Durfort mansion, Emma had prepared meals for congressmen, plantation owners, even the mayor of Richmond. But she'd never known Monsieur to get this worked up about a dinner.

"Yes, Monsieur has given me the menu. He wants to start with oyster stew and pickled okra for the first course. After that, they'll have broiled pheasant and ham with candied yams. For dessert, he wants cherry pie and tipsy cake."

Emma shook her head. "Warren, how in the hell am I supposed to get all that food by tomorrow?"

The butler nodded. "I'll have two of the footmen fetch the food for you. Tell them what you need."

"You best give them a pretty penny, too. That food's not coming cheap."

"Any shopkeeper in Richmond will extend credit to Monsieur Durfort."

"Yeah, if Monsieur would get his ass in that shop himself," she said. "But they're not going to trust one of your coal-faced footmen asking for credit."

"You're right," Warren said, rubbing his chin. "I'll draft a note."

"And get Monsieur to sign it, too. It's not like you're some big wig either."

Huffing, the butler left the kitchen. He'd need to write promissory notes for the footmen – and still find a seamstress to alter Mademoiselle's wedding dress.

***

Two days later, the butler led Harriet Hemings into the mansion's second-floor parlor. "Mademoiselle will be in shortly. Is there anything you need for the fitting?"

"No, sir. Thank you. I have everything I need," Harriet said, tapping her sewing bag.

After the butler left, Harriet looked around the room. Like the rest of the three-story mansion, the room was lavishly furnished with silk upholstered furniture, intricately carved doors, velvet drapes, and rich carpets. This was nothing like the simplicity she'd known at Monticello.

For a moment, Harriet felt a pang of longing for her childhood. Being near her mother had been a comfort, despite being in bondage. Now, they were both free but had moved apart, looking for work.

The parlor door opened and Mademoiselle Claudia entered. She was tall and fair, with green eyes. "You are Harriet?" she said in English with a heavy accent.

"Je parle un peu français," Harriet said.

Her face brightening into a smile, the bride-to-be replied in French. "I'm delighted to hear that. Only Andrei and the butler speak French here. This is wonderful!"

Harriet nodded. "Just please speak slowly, miss."

"Of course. Where did you learn our language?"

Harriet hesitated, unsure how to answer. There was no polite way to explain her mother's trips to

Paris with Master Jefferson. "I learned in a home where I was in service," she finally said.

"How fortunate for me," Claudia said. She then walked to a corner and opened a chest. "This is the wedding gown I was given by Andrei's family," she said, taking out the garment. "What do you think of it?"

Harriet looked over the garish dress. Along with too many bows, ruffles and layers of lace, the waist was unfashionably high. She might be fired, but Harriet sensed Miss Claudia would want to hear the truth. "This garment, miss..." she said, shaking her head, "It's going to need a lot of work."

"You're right, Harriet. I think Andrei's family meant to embarrass me."

"Why would they do that?"

"I was not their first choice for his wife," Claudia said, then laughed. "Or even their second. They wanted a daughter-in-law who would be more... reserved."

Harriet met her eyes and smiled, then picked up the gown. "I think we can remove some of the frills and take down the waist, miss," she said.

For the next half-hour they spoke excitedly about ways to improve the gown.

After they'd finished, Claudia took Harriet's hands. "I hope we can be friends."

"I don't think that would be appropriate, miss," Harriet said looking at the floor.

"Why not?"

"That's not the way things are here. I'm free but I'm colored."

"But you're no darker than some of my cousins."

"People here don't see things that simply."

"Well, people here can change their minds,"

Claudia said. "Would you come to work here as my personal attendant?"

The decision was easy. Harriet's work as a seamstress barely made ends meet. "Yes, miss. I can do that."

Over the next 37 years, Harriet Hemings would become part of Claudia Durfort's household, first as her lady's maid, and later as the nanny of her children who were raised in Paris.

~=~

PARIS, FRANCIA

Hassan and I were quiet on the eCAB ride back to Hotel Durant.

I tried to doze in the car, but it was useless. Ludolph's betrayal should not have been surprising, but it stung all the same. Measuring your worth by the opinion of a man was a sucker's game. But women did it anyway, even with a louse like Eltz.

There was a bright side, though. I'd reached a parity of power with Hassan. We were both armed now. I was still in danger, but my chances of surviving had improved.

Once we were inside the hotel room, I faced Hassan. "I'm ready to make the call," I said, holding out my hand for his phone.

Hassan's fingers danced over the touchpad as he unlocked the mobile. He then held up the device. "The phone is set on speaker mode. I'll need to listen to the call. Agreed?"

"No," I said. If Hassan heard Dot's voice, he would know she was a woman. The less Hassan knew about Dot the better.

"I need to be sure your asset is cooperating, Olivia," he said. "You can tell her I'm listening to the call. I don't need to know her name."

I was stunned – but tried to hide it. "What makes you think my asset is a woman?"

"Pronouns," Hassan said. "You've worked very hard to avoid giving me a gender. You wouldn't have done that if your asset was a man," he said, then added, "I also suspect she's in the military. You probably met her while you were in uniform."

Hassan was clever. I had to give him that. "All right. You can listen," I said, extending my hand.

Hassan nodded and gave up the phone.

I held the mobile for a moment. Making the call was a triumph – but a hollow one. My life was ruined – and probably Dot's as well.

All we could hope for now was to survive.

I took a deep breath and dialed her number.

The phone rang nearly a dozen times before Dot answered. Her voice sounded stern. "Who is this?" she asked, no doubt suspicious about a call from an unknown number in late evening.

"It's OJ," I said. "Can you talk?"

Her voice brighter, Dot said, "Yeah. What's up, sister?"

"Sorry to drop this on you. I've been burned by the SS and they could be coming after you."

"When did it happen?"

"About six hours ago. This is the first chance I've had to call you. And there's one other thing you need to know... This line is secure but someone else is listening to this call. It's too complicated to explain right now. But don't give away your name, understand?"

"Roger that."

"You need to lay low for a while – at least until we're sure you're not implicated."

"I've got some leave I haven't used. This might be the time."

"Good," I said, then added, "Look, before you cut out, there's something I need to ask."

"Whatever it is, you've got it."

"I need to know everyone in Francia who authorized the delivery of the bloom to Virginia – and I need to know soon."

"That's above my paygrade, OJ. But I can probably dig up the shipping orders on the bloom sent to Charlottesville. That should tell us who sent it."

"Can you do that from home?"

"No. I'll have to go back on base and log into DEFNET."

"Don't go back there. It's too risky."

"I know you wouldn't ask if it wasn't important. I'll go right now."

"It's after ten there. Someone's going to get suspicious."

"I can handle this. Trust me, sister," Dot said. "Can I call you back on this number?"

I looked at Hassan. He nodded in agreement. "Yes," I said.

"I'll get back to you ASAP."

"You're a beast, girl. Thank you," I said and ended the call.

Turning toward Hassan, I handed him the phone, my hands tingling. Since the shock of my arrest, my goal had been to warn Dot. Whatever happened now, I'd met my duty. Then I remembered another threat to my comrade. "After she calls back, I'll delete her number from your phone."

"Like I said, I have no interest in exposing your friend, Olivia. The media in Francia wouldn't take a Britannic source seriously."

"You said that with some respect this time."

"What I said about her before was stupid. I'm sorry."

Buoyed by his remorse, I said, "I could use a smoke. You have any cigarettes left?"

"There are still some in my other jacket," he said, walking across the room. After fishing through the pockets of the garment on the bed, he pulled out a near-empty pack of Admirals. "I need to get more cigarettes," he said. "What flavor of vape do you use? I'll have room service bring up both."

"Keep it simple. Just get more Admirals," I said. I didn't want to admit it. But I was growing fond of the old school cigs.

***

Dorothy Leigh Blake ended the call and put the mobile back into the jacket pocket of her pantsuit. Leaving the parking lot, she walked back inside the restaurant. Her date looked up, smiling expectantly, as Dot returned to their table.

"I'm sorry, Barbara. I've got to go," she said, touching her date's shoulder.

Barbara shrugged away from Dot's hand. "This is a shitty way of ditching me," she whispered.

Dot had met Barbara through an online dating service catering to gay women. The forum offered a measure of privacy to a group that was persecuted in Virginia. This dinner was their first time to meet IRL – in real life.

"I'm not ditching you. You've got some serious charm vibes, girl," Dot said, leaning close, keeping her voice low. "But there's something important I have to do. It can't wait."

Barbara looked around nervously. Making a scene could be dangerous. "Then I'll see you again?"

Dot sighed. She knew that was unlikely. If OJ had been burned, Dot would need to go underground. Her date did not deserve a lie that would only hurt more later. "Please understand, Barbara. This has nothing to do with you," she said, then put a fifty from her wallet on the table. "Stay and finish dinner. I have to go."

Without stopping at home for her uniform, Dot left the restaurant for the base.

Driving through the late evening traffic, the shock of OJ's news wore away. In its place rose the consequences.

Dot had struggled to overcome the hurdles of race and gender to become an army officer. Her rank, her privileges, her pension, all of it was at risk now.

But she'd gone into this op with open eyes. As a precaution, she'd withdrawn two months' pay from her bank account and added the cash to the "lifeboat" in her apartment – a small suitcase with clothes, sundries and a .38 snub-nose. If it came to that, Dot hoped it would be enough to reach her grandmother's kin in Georgia.

Maybe worst of all, she and OJ would probably never meet again.

OJ was the only Army officer who knew she was gay. On a spur of the moment, Dot had come out to OJ when the two were alone during a break in their combat training at VMI.

"So, I thought you ought to know," she'd said, scraping the mud off her boots. "I'm into women. I hope that won't change things between us."

"Hell, no. That just says you trust me."

OJ's answer convinced Dot her impulse had been right.

When Dot stopped her car at the base's main gate, the night shift guard looked puzzled. Not too many women in civvies turned up at this hour. But after checking her CAC card, the guard raised the gate, saluted and said, "You're good to go, Major."

Driving into the base, Dot now realized getting the C-4 shipped to Caen might have been the easy part of OJ's op with the Germans. Dot had sent a requisition for the explosives to the Charlottesville armory for a fake unit of demolition engineers that would blow up bridges deep inside the borders of Virginia in case of a retreat. With all the ordinance orders flying around in the pre-war preparations, as Dot expected, no one had bothered to validate her request.

Getting the information OJ wanted about the bloom might pose a bigger risk. So be it. She'd given her word to help OJ.

Dot parked her car and scanned her division's building, one of eight identical two-story structures on the base. The light coming from the windows was dim. The MP vehicles that patrolled the base weren't in sight. But leaving her car in the parking lot would certainly draw them inside. She'd have to work fast.

Like most senior officers, Dot had an entry code for after-hours access. But once inside the building, she headed directly to her boss's office instead of her personal workspace. Dot was sure any information about bloom was Top Secret – and only the general commanding her division had that level of access.

Dot did not turn on the light after entering the general's office. She knew the space quite well. As the only female senior officer, the general often asked Dot to file his personal readiness reports when he wanted to play golf. The asshole often told Dot she should be honored by this privilege.

But there was one saving grace to this patronizing arrangement. She knew the password to the general's computer – and that gave her Top Secret access to DEFNET.

After logging into DEFNET, she checked on the classified shipments into the armory in Charlottesville. There was only one in the last six months. The contents of the shipment were redacted but the sender was not. This had to be it.

Dot read the information on the sender twice, then repeated it to herself with her eyes closed. After committing it to memory, she closed the DEFNET connection. While shutting down the computer, she heard footsteps in the hallway. Then the office lights went on.

"What are you doing here?" a voice behind her said.

Dot turned and saw an MP sergeant, his sidearm drawn.

"Put away the hardware before someone gets hurt, sergeant. I work here," she said calmly.

"Get your hands up," he said, the gun still leveled.

Dot lifted her palms. "My CAC is in my pocket," she said, nodding toward her jacket.

"Show me," he said without lowering his weapon, "But do it real slow, lady."

Dot slowly took out her wallet and held out her military identification card.

After peering at the CAC, the MP said, "Major Baker, what are you doing on the computer in General Holt's office?"

"Getting work done for the general."

"With the lights out?"

"That's how I prefer to work, sergeant. I don't like the glare on the screen."

"I wasn't told you'd be here," the MP said. His gun was lowered but still not in its holster.

"It's a last minute assignment from the general. Top Secret."

"Can you show me your orders?" he said, holstering his weapon.

Dot smiled. "Generals don't write up orders, sergeant. They bark and you jump."

"Sorry, Major. You'll have to do better than that."

"All right. Call the general yourself," Dot said. "He's in Paris right now and it's 0400 hours there. Feel free to wake him up."

The MP squirmed. "I'm not going to do that, ma'am," he said, grabbing her arm. " But you'll have to come to my HQ until we can sort this out."

Dot could not let that happen. OJ would never know who shipped the bloom if she was taken into custody. As the MP hustled her down the hallway, Dot sidekicked the sergeant below the knee. The soldier went down with a groan of pain.

Before the sergeant could rise, Dot delivered a knifehand strike to the back of his neck. The blow to his carotid sinus left him unconscious.

Dot ran to the exit and looked outside. There were no other MPs in the area. She walked slowly to her car, careful not to appear furtive.

Once she was off the base, Dot pulled to the side of the road. She didn't have much time. The MP had her name and rank. Once he came to, the police would be dispatched to her apartment. She'd need to pick up her lifeboat before they arrived. But first, she needed to complete her mission.

Dot pulled the phone from her pocket and redialed OJ's number.

***

The room service porter handed Brody a tray with four packs of Admirals and a disposable lighter. The man's eyes widened at Brody's generous tip.

"Thank you, *monsieur*," the porter said before leaving.

Brody handed two of the cigarette packs and the lighter to Olivia. "Admirals are one of the best things about your country. I'm surprised you find them quaint."

Olivia tore the cellophane off one of the packs. "I'm surprised you buy the product of an enemy," she said, then opened the wrapper, took out a cigarette, and lit it.

Brody fired up his own Admiral. "It's a guilty pleasure."

Cigarette dangling from her lips, Olivia dropped into the chair by the window, took off her shoes and began massaging her feet. "Can your per diem handle something to drink?" she said, nodding toward the mini bar.

"Sure," Brody said. "They might have Pernod."

"You've done your homework, Hassan," she said, walking to the mini bar in her bare feet. Olivia then opened the cabinet and took out a shooter bottle of Pernod. "Is there anything about me you don't know?"

"You'd do the same in my place, I expect."

Olivia twisted off the cap on the Pernod and took a long pull. "Obviously, you've read a dossier on me. But I don't know anything about you."

"Whatever you know about me makes you a threat, Olivia. I don't want that to happen."

"Relax, Hassan. I'm not talking about anything meaningful," she said, then downed another long swallow. "I could use a distraction. I'm worried about my friend in Virginia."

"All right. Go ahead and ask."

"Let's see," she said tapping her chin. "I'm guessing you've never been married."

"You're right."

"Why would you? Men who look like you have no trouble finding women."

"I'm going to take that as a compliment."

"Being coy doesn't suit you," she said. "I'm curious about your looks, though. I'm sure your real name is not Hassan – and you're not from the Middle East. I'd say you have Britannic ancestors who are white, black and native. Not sure about the ratio, though."

"You left out Asian."

"Asian?

"My great-great grandfather was a Chinese seaman on a British ship. The shipping company he worked for went bankrupt and he got stranded in Philadelphia," he said. "What about you? Anyone like me hiding in your woodpile?"

"My family's been in Virginia a long time," she said. "Since the Jamestown settlement, actually."

"Ah, Tidewater aristocrats – and all of them white as rice, I'm sure."

"Well, we're distantly related to Jefferson – through his daughter Martha. But I've met some of our Sally Hemings kin," she said, thinking of Dot.

"Not many folks from your class in Virginia would admit that," Brody said, "or associate with any tawny relatives."

"I won't deny some Tidewater families can be narrow-minded."

"So what made yours different?"

"Our family is military," she said. "My father used to say that when your life's on the line, you measure people by their courage, not their color."

"Where's your father now?"

"Dead."

"I'm sorry," Brody said, lowering his eyes. "I suspect he died fighting pennies."

"He did. My brother, too."

Brody walked to the mini bar and took out a cognac single. He opened the bottle and raised it in a toast. "To soldiers and their families. Grief doesn't take sides."

They both nodded and took a drink.

Staring at the small cognac bottle, Brody said, "It must have been a hard choice for you, taking up with the Germans and keeping secrets from your embassy."

"What I've done with the Germans is to save lives in Virginia," she said. "My loyalty is to my country, not some sellout politicians sucking up to the toads to make themselves richer."

"I get that," Brody said, nodding. "We have party members in Pennsylvania who preach equality but live like kings."

"Oh? Sounds like we might have a closet dissident here."

"I don't think *any* country lives up to the bullshit they spout on patriotic holidays. But I still—"

Brody's cell phone buzzed.

After looking at the display, he said, "Your friend in Virginia is calling." As Brody handed her the phone, he realized his intimate talk with Olivia had distracted him. For a moment, he'd forgotten Jim Easley's deadline. Pennsylvania's raid on the armory in Charlottesville was less than twenty-four hours away. His time to prevent a war was running out.

***

I could hear the excitement in Dot's voice over the cellphone speaker. She was a warrior, always stirred by the challenge of a mission. "The bloom was shipped to Charlottesville by General Regis Lafoy," she said. "He's a two-star in the 3rd Marine Infantry Regiment. Their HQ is in Vannes."

"Never heard of him," I said, then looked at Hassan. He shook his head, then began jotting the information on a hotel notepad.

"That's not surprising," Dot said. "If sending the bloom is a skunk works op, they wouldn't use anyone with a high-profile," she said, then added. "I have a phone number for the 3rd Marines' Headquarters on the shipping orders. Would that help?"

Hassan touched my arm and nodded.

"Yes," I said into the phone.

Dot recited the number, then said, "That's all I have. Sorry I couldn't be more helpful."

"One more thing... Be sure you destroy any documents that tie you to the C-4 shipment."

"Don't worry. It's already done."

"Thank you, sister. You've gone above and beyond," I said. "Now get your ass out of there."

After a long pause, Dot said, "Never, never die."

The verse from the VMI fight song made my throat catch. "Never, never die," I said, my voice fading as I ended the call.

I stared at the phone. For more than a decade, Dot and I had shared a dream of reforming Virginia's military. Now, we'd probably never speak again.

"Go ahead and delete her number," Hassan said softly.

"Right," I said, erasing Dot's number from the phone. Handing the mobile back to Hassan, I felt unburdened. I'd done right by my comrade. But now, I faced a moment of truth with Hassan.

I slowly backed away a few steps. "You got what you wanted. What happens now?" I said, prepared to draw the Glock in my pocket.

"You've done all you can, Olivia," he said. Then, very slowly, he took out his wallet. "Here," he said, peeling out a half-dozen 10,000-franc notes. "There's a dry-cleaning shop at 53 Rue LeClair. Tell them you're picking up a trench coat for Pierre Humbolt. For twenty-five-thousand francs, they'll fix you up with the papers to get out of Francia."

My mouth gaped. "Why are you doing this?" The best I'd expected was to walk away alive.

"You may not be an ally. But you're no longer an enemy," he said. "Stay in this room until morning. The dry-cleaning shop will be open by then. I've got to go."

I had not expected this. "Why are you leaving?" I asked. Now that Hassan no longer posed a threat, staying with him a while longer seemed useful.

"It's nearly midnight in Pennsylvania. I need to contact my superiors and report what I've learned about Lafoy."

"You stay and make the call," I said, putting on my shoes. "I'll go for a walk."

"That won't work. I'll need my bureau's help following Lafoy up the food chain. There's no telling how long that call might take."

"Look, Hassan. I know the people inside the government of Francia better than anyone you have back home. You'll have a better chance of finding Lafoy's connection to the prime minister with my help."

"You're right," he admitted. "But why would you do that?"

"You're funding my escape. I'd like to earn my keep," I said, then added, "Besides, I want to get even with those SS motherfuckers."

"If you help me, Francia will stop providing bloom to Virginia."

"That was one of my goals too, remember?" I said, moving toward the door. "Call in your report. I'll take a walk and when I'm back, we can figure out who's pulling Lafoy's strings."

"There's an all-night coffee shop two blocks north. Expresso and croissants sound good?" he asked, handing me some smaller franc notes from his pocket.

"Roger that," I said and left the room.

***

The telephone on the nightstand rang.

Nestled against her husband on the bed, Claire Easley lifted her head from the pillow. "I know it's not for me at this hour," she said before picking up the phone and handing it to him.

Yawning, Jim Easley got out of bed and carried the cordless telephone out of the bedroom.

Entering their living room, he walked past the family bible displayed under glass on the shelf. He'd put it there as a reminder. Never forget what you owed to those who'd passed.

Easley dropped into a chair. "Yeah?" he said into the receiver.

"Boss, I've got the first link in the chain," the familiar voice said.

"I *know* that, Brody," he said, irritated by the pointless call. "We're tracing the number you called in Virginia about two hours ago. Our people should know who it is by morning."

"Forget that lead, boss. It's a dead end."

"What?"

"I've uncovered a toad two-star who authorized the bloom shipment into Charlottesville. His name is Regis Lafoy. He's stationed with the 3rd Marines in Vannes."

"That's a good start, son. But we need more," Easley said. "One of our Communications people has teed up the story off-the-record with a reporter at *Le Figaro*. The media's hot for anything on *munitions biologique* and her editor is willing to run a front-page piece. But we need to connect the conspiracy to the prime minister."

"I understand," Brody said. "I checked out Lafoy on the database I can access on my phone before calling you. I came up empty. Can you send me whatever we have on Lafoy in Philly?"

"I doubt it'll be much, but I'll call and get the night shift working on that. They'll text you whatever they can find."

"Thanks, boss."

"What makes you think the number we traced earlier is a dead end? We're already staging the choppers and a special forces team to storm the armory. I'd hate to overlook a lead that could stop a war."

"You'll have to trust me, boss."

"All right, you cocky bastard," he said. "You've got less than 12 hours. Go do what you do."

***

After his call to Jim Easley, Brody walked to the bathroom sink and splashed cold water on his face. Less than six hours of sleep in the last three days was catching up with him – and there was more left to do. His attraction to Olivia was not helping. He needed to focus.

Drying off, he heard a knock on the door and let Olivia into the room.

"Done with your call?" she asked, carrying a white paper bag.

Brody nodded. "I'm expecting a text with more background on Lafoy."

"Good, that might be helpful," she said, taking the coffees and croissants out of the bag and placing them on the mini bar. "I've got a plan for making Lafoy tell us who ordered him to ship the bloom."

"Really?" Brody said with a smirk. "What took you so long?"

Olivia's face darkened. "Fuck you, Hassan," she said. "Do you want my help or not?"

"I don't recall asking for it."

"I thought you were smart. My mistake," she said, heading for the door.

Brody held up his palms. Olivia might be helpful, he realized. She had him tied in knots. "All right. Wait," he said. "Neither of us has had much rest. Maybe we're a bit on edge."

Olivia exhaled slowly. "An apology might help."

"I'm sorry, Olivia," he said. "I was being an asshole."

"Well, then. Have some coffee, asshole," she said, handing him a cup. "It might help your mood."

After a gulp of brew, Brody said, "So what's your plan for cracking Lafoy?"

"I had time to think about Lafoy while I was walking," she said. "I don't know him, but I know his type of soldier. The Army of Virginia has way too many of them. Officers like Lafoy rise through the ranks faster than most. Some of them court politicians and others have family connections. What they have in common is a willingness to whore their uniforms to get ahead," she said. "And what they fear most is getting caught screwing up by a superior."

"I get what you're saying. But how do we find out Lafoy's superior in the conspiracy?"

"First, we'll need to make a guess about who that is," she said, then walked to the desk and picked up the hotel notepad. "I'm going to start by making a list of everyone I know in toad military circles close to the prime minister," she said, then began writing a name on each sheet of the notepad. "Why don't you have something to eat? The croissants are good," she said over her shoulder.

By the time Brody had finished his pastry, Olivia had over a dozen note sheets spread out on the bed. Each had a name and the official's title.

"I've arranged them in order of proximity to the prime minister," she said, pointing at the notes divided into three rows. "The ones at the top are the people closest to the PM."

"Are you sure about that?"

"Yes."

"Then throw out everyone in the bottom two rows."

"Why?"

"Conspiracies stay small," he said. "Whoever pulled Lafoy's strings was someone very close to the prime minister."

Olivia nodded. "That makes sense," she said, clearing away all but four note sheets. "Let's see who we have left."

"The defense minister looks promising," Brody said, pointing to the sheet for Alain Ricard.

"No, Ricard is known for being non-partisan," she said, removing his note. "The PM wouldn't trust him."

"Well, that leaves us with the liaison to the joint chiefs of staff, the national security adviser, and the director of national intelligence."

"It's got to be Helen Levet," she said, picking up the note for the national security adviser. "She's the only civilian – and I've heard she has political ambitions."

"Are you sure?" Brody asked. "We'll only get one chance."

"My gut tells me she's the one. The others are bureaucrats."

"Then that works for me," Brody said. "Now what's the rest of your plan?"

"I presume you can fake a Virginia accent in French?"

"*C'est très sûr, madame*," Brody said, with a perfect Tidewater lilt.

"Good," she said, then explained the details of her sting on Lafoy.

When Olivia was finished, Brody said, "That's pretty devious for someone who's never worked in covert ops."

Olivia managed a smile. "Desperation can be inspiring."

"Look," Brody said, rubbing his neck. "There's not much more either of us can do until morning. We can't call Lafoy at his base before then. Why don't we both get some sleep? You take the bed. I'll stretch out on the floor."

***

I covered my mouth, stifling a yawn. "Getting some rest makes sense, Hassan," I said. "But you don't need to be gallant. There's room for two on the bed – just don't assume it's an invitation to anything else."

Hassan smiled. "Trust me, Olivia. I'm as tired as you are."

Before long, we were both stretched out on the bed, fully clothed under separate blankets.

When Hassan's breathing grew slow and regular, I knew he'd fallen asleep. Despite my exhaustion, I was wide awake.

Memories of the night's frantic events came rushing back... my arrest at *Le Velour Bleu*... discovering Hassan was a PRP agent... mugging the john... my arrest by the police... the chase through Montmartre... learning Eltz wanted me dead... never seeing Dot again...

Nothing remained of the life I'd known before – and I was completely alone.

Hassan stirred in the bed, breaking my chain of thoughts. I could tell by his breathing that he was still asleep. The nearness of his body brought another reminder... If not for Hassan's courage and wits, the SS would already have me in custody.

Lying in the dark, listening to Hassan breathing, my mind wandered to a place I'd never imagined... making love to him.

***

Bernard lifted his face from the grass, his head throbbing violently. He touched the back of his skull and felt a painful pair of bumps. Trying to rise from the dewy ground, he staggered and vomited instead. With the dark shapes of the park around him spinning, Bernard crawled to the base of a tree and hugged it to steady him. As the dizziness began to pass, his memory returned.

What kind of game was Eltz playing? Instead of picking up the location for the hit, he'd been ambushed. None of this added up. But one thing was clear: Eltz had made him look like a chump. Bernard could not let that pass. A thing like this could hurt his reputation. He was *Le Fleurist*, the guy you called when you wanted to see flowers at a funeral.

Then he remembered the audition.

"God damn that German prick," Bernard muttered as he rose unsteadily to his feet. He'd have to wear a knit cap to cover the bumps on his head after he got cleaned up for the audition. That might cost him the part. You never knew with directors.

Walking slowly out of the park, Bernard made a vow. It was bad for business to kill a client. But after his audition, *Le Fleurist* would pay a visit to Ludolph Eltz and put the fear of God into him.

1868

HARPER'S FERRY, VIRGINIA

Squeezing her large hoop skirt through the narrow doorway, Pauline Savari stepped out of the train's last passenger car.

The Harper's Ferry rail station looked like most rural stops on her journey over the last two months: a small wooden building, its roof extending over the passenger platform. But this station had a notable addition.

A few steps beyond the platform stood a guard hut with a sign that read: VIRGINIA BORDER AUTHORITY.

"If you are continuing into Virginia, please form a line at the Border Authority door," the conductor called out, pointing toward the hut.

As one of the last passengers to leave the train, Pauline found herself near the end of the queue.

The line moved slowly as the passengers were

brought into the guard hut one at a time. After more than forty minutes in the summer heat, Pauline was finally allowed to enter.

Inside, she found an army captain at a small table. Beside him stood a corporal, rifle slung over his shoulder.

The captain held out his palm without looking up. "May I see proof of your nationality?"

Pauline handed him the passport in her purse.

The soldier put down the document, reached into his tunic and retrieved a pipe and a pouch of tobacco. He filled the pipe and lit it, took a few puffs, then picked up the passport.

"I see you're from Francia, Miss Savari," he said, pipe clenched in his teeth. "What's your reason for traveling to Virginia?"

"I'm here to write a book about the region."

The captain put down his pipe and scoffed. "I can't imagine people in Francia would much care about matters around here."

Pauline managed a smile. "I'm afraid my editor shares your opinion."

That conversation four months earlier was etched into her memory.

Her editor had snickered when Pauline explained her idea for a book about the Britannic region. "Do you really want to cross an ocean to write about those bumpkins?"

"You said the imprint was hungry for fresh stories."

"Yes, but you're a woman. Why not write about the soirees of Napoleon III? Our readers don't care about those backward people."

"I'll write a book that will make them care." Being the publisher's niece made her case more persuasive.

"Then, go," the editor said, raising his hands in surrender.

The captain coughed and picked up his pipe again. "Do you have any other form of identification?" he asked, emptying the pipe's ashes onto the floor.

"I should think my passport is sufficient."

"I'm afraid not," he said, sounding bored. "Have the porter take your luggage off the train for inspection."

"Captain, I crossed the border from Massachusetts to New York and then into Pennsylvania without this kind of bother."

"Ma'am, Virginia was invaded by Pennsylvania four years ago. Our side is not going to let down its guard again."

Pauline sighed. This man was a soldier, but he was no different than the other low-level government officials she'd encountered so far on her journey through the Britannic nations. They all expected bribes.

"May I buy a meal for some of your men?" she said, then reached into her purse and held out a five-franc note.

The captain's lips curled. "My men are hungrier than that."

After Pauline doubled the bribe, the captain flipped his wrist, waving her through.

The train crossed the Harper's Ferry bridge over the Potomac and took Pauline to the end of the line in Charlottesville. There, she boarded a horse-drawn coach. A few hours into the journey, they emerged from miles of wooded foothills into flat, dry farmland.

A plume of dust trailed the carriage as it trundled past a patchwork of tiny plots, each with a battered shack near its center. A few homes had crude pens with scrawny livestock. Most of the people working the farms were negroes.

"What are these farmers growing?" Pauline asked the minister who had shared the coach with her since Charlottesville.

"Tobacco, mostly," the minister said. "But these aren't farmers, ma'am. They're sharecroppers."

"How is that different?"

"Farmers own their land. These folks work the land for someone else and get a share of the harvest. A lot of them used to be slaves."

"Who owns the land?"

"Nine times out of ten, it's a Tidewater family – or a rich toad." The minister lowered his eyes, realizing he'd insulted the young woman. "Sorry, ma'am. You speak English so well, I forgot you was from Francia."

"I had a nanny from Virginia. I learned English from her," Pauline said, remembering Harriet Hemings.

Pauline's mother had brought Harriet to Paris as her lady's maid. When Pauline was born, Harriet became her wet nurse and nanny. The first words she'd heard in English were at Harriet's breast. As Pauline grew, Harriet taught her more than English. She inspired Pauline with her compassion, duty and dignity. Harriet remained in service with Pauline's family until her last days. In fact, it was Harriet's passing last year that had inspired Pauline to write about the region.

A new sight outside the window caught Pauline's eye: a field lined with furrows of tall plants with straight stalks. "What kind of crop is that?" she asked the minister.

"That's corn, ma'am," the minister said. "The Indians grow it."

Looking beyond the field, Pauline saw a group of houses. "Is that where they live?"

"Yes, that's an Indian village. Monocan, most likely."

Pauline had read about the Indians of New Francia. She'd expected the natives to live in hide-covered huts. But this village looked like most of the others she'd seen in the territory. All the same, she was concerned. "Are we in any danger here?" she asked the minister.

"Now, don't you worry, miss," he said. "We haven't had any Indian trouble for quite a while around here. In fact, the only trouble we've had is getting them to baptize the young'uns they've had with whites. There's plenty of them around."

The minister's words fit her observations. Most of the Britannic people she'd seen had complexions that ranged from maple to mahogany.

Her curiosity satisfied, Pauline returned to studying the notes for her upcoming interview, the most consequential of her trip. She would soon meet the man who had ended slavery in North America.

The sound of the horse's hooves grew louder as the coach entered a cobblestone road.

Looking outside, Pauline was surprised by the sight. They were approaching a grassy bluff with a compound of multi-story brick buildings with colonnaded fronts. Four smaller structures edged a larger building with a graceful central tower. Evidently, this handsome campus was Washington College.

Ushered by a student, Pauline entered the college president's office where she sat on one of two settees flanking a low table. After a few minutes, Robert E. Lee, the former Field Marshal of the Army of Virginia, entered the room.

"Welcome Miss Savari," Lee said, with a courtly nod. "I hope your coach ride from Charlottesville was not too strenuous."

"I've become quite used to riding coaches, General."

Lee pressed his palms together. "If you don't mind, I prefer not to be addressed by my former military rank. I'm an educator now."

"Of course, sir," Pauline said, dipping her chin. "Thank you for agreeing to see me."

"I must confess," Lee said. "I don't get many requests for interviews by authors from Francia."

After a few more rounds of pleasantries, Pauline drew the notepad from her purse. "Shall we begin our interview?

Lee nodded. "Certainly."

"Liberating your slaves was a singular act of courage, sir. What prompted your decision to free them?

Lee rubbed his lips. "The war with Pennsylvania pitted us against a more powerful foe. Our enemy had annexed three of their neighboring nations and we could not match their manpower. To avoid being conquered, I gave my servants fit for military duty the opportunity to become freemen if they joined the troops under my command."

"Other slaveholders in Virginia followed your example. Did you expect that?"

"I did not consult with the Tidewater families before making my decision," Lee said. "But when the troops under my command showed their mettle and we won a string of battles, other landowners saw the virtue of this move."

"The decision to free your slaves ultimately led to the abolition of slavery in all Britannic nations. Can you tell me how that happened?"

"The abolition of our peculiar institution was not my goal," Lee said. "But in the end, it prevented greater turmoil."

Pauline was surprised by his reply. "I don't understand."

"Our negro troops fought honorably in defense of our native soil against the invaders from Pennsylvania. But that changed once the tide of the war turned in our favor and we entered enemy territory," Lee said. "At the battle of Gettysburg in Pennsylvania, over half of our negro troops deserted."

"I didn't know that," Pauline confessed.

"Yes, they betrayed Virginia when we needed them most."

"Could these troops have fled because they were in a nation without plantation slavery?"

Lee raised his palm. "Regardless of the reason, those deserters created a dangerous upheaval that took years to quell," he said. "You see, news of all those negroes running wild in Pennsylvania led to masses of slaves escaping north in Virginia, the Carolinas and even Georgia."

"What happened then?"

Lee's mouth curled into the hint of a smile. "The flood of negroes heading north forced Pennsylvania and the other northern nations to end their domestic slavery. With a horde of blacks suddenly on their doorstep, those nations faced the prospect of a negro revolt from their own slaves."

"I presume that same fear of a negro uprising spread to all the Britannic nations."

"It was a sensible decision," Lee said, nodding. "White slaveholders have always been a minority in this region."

"Did the end of slavery ruin the slaveholders?"

"Yes... at first. But we found ways to avoid a total disaster. White families still owned most of the land. Our former slaves found a new life working those same fields as freemen."

Pauline's face hardened. "With the landholders taking most of the profits."

"We reward hard work in Virginia. We're not like Pennsylvania."

"What do you mean?"

"The government of Pennsylvania wastes its resources on handouts to the idle. The only way they know to acquire new wealth is through conquest."

"In fairness, I've traveled through Pennsylvania and Virginia. Both countries seem impoverished to me, sir."

"Pennsylvania controls the lives of its citizens under the cudgel of the common good. Their people must submit to whatever the government decrees."

"Yet, the end result is the same. Both nations remain poor."

"In Virginia, our people are free to choose their way of life."

"Until recently, only whites were free in Virginia. Isn't that right?"

Lee leaned back in his chair, knitting his fingers. "I'm surprised you traveled all this way to impugn your host."

"I didn't travel here to flatter you, sir. I came here searching for the truth."

Lee rose to his feet. "I'll have someone show you to the door," he said coldly, then walked out of the room.

Stunned, Pauline gathered her notes. She'd hoped to find Robert E. Lee had ended slavery through an act of benevolence. Instead, she'd discovered Lee had traded one form of exploitation for another.

After leaving the university, Pauline began the last leg of her journey.

Over the next three months, she travelled through North Carolina, South Carolina and Georgia.

North Carolina, like Virginia, was sustained by tobacco. Most of the tobacco fields were owned by the heirs of lords granted lands by the British crown over 200 years before. Their feckless stewardship of the land was exploited by Franks – much like Virginia.

In South Carolina, a dynasty based on rice had crumbled, its exports to Francia displaced by cheaper rice from Asia. An experiment there growing cotton had failed. Removing the seeds from the bolls proved too costly.

Georgia had begun as a chamber pot for petty criminals from England. The nation's primary resource was its pine trees, used for pitch, tar and rosin on sailing ships. Unfortunately, the export of these products fetched meager profits.

Although most Britannic nations differed in the font of their economies, they were similar in their common misery.

During her long journey back to Paris, Pauline began a summary of her observations. Her conclusions about this region were disturbing – and revealing.

Even the poorest people in Francia lived better than most of the unfortunate souls in this region. The cause was not hard to find.

Francia's heavy hands were everywhere. The owners of the coal mines, railroads, banks and shipping companies were all Franks. Her countrymen had a stranglehold on every major industry. Pauline was ashamed that her grandfather, Andrei Durfort, had been one of them.

The only exception to Francia's dominance was agriculture in Virginia and North Carolina. There, a few plantation families still clung to their estates, their land now parsed out to sharecroppers. While slavery had been abolished, many of those once enslaved endured a new form of servitude.

There was only one path for the landless to acquire wealth in this region: join the government and gain access to graft and bribes.

Over the last decade, a fresh surge of immigrants from Europe had arrived in Quebec and New Orleans looking for a better life in New Francia's undeveloped west. Most of these migrants shunned the Britannic countries. They offered no hope for new land, no prospects for jobs, no thriving markets for the industrious.

Her travels in the Britannic region had left Pauline with a distressing conclusion. It became the title of her book: A LESSER LAND.

After her return to Paris, Pauline handed the final draft of the manuscript to her editor. Two weeks later, they met to discuss the book.

"This is very good work, Pauline," her editor said. "We'll publish it before year's end."

A number of scholars praised the work. Their accolades did little for book sales, however. Copies languished on the shelves.

It seemed the busy people of Paris had little interest

in a book about a backwater region half a world away they believed was peopled by savages, negroes and the crude flotsam of Europe.

***

PHILADELPHIA, PENNSYLVANIA

Eustace Easley walked past the small shops along Philadelphia's Broad Street with an urgent stride, a bible tucked under his arm.

Four years ago, he'd been in awe the first time he looked through the windows of the barbershop, bakery, shoe shop and grocery store on the street. From the look of it, all these businesses had colored owners. The idea was beyond his imagination.

Eustace had arrived in Philadelphia after traveling over 140 miles from Gettysburg, walking at night and hiding during the day. That had been the easiest part of his journey from Virginia.

It began the day Master Easley rounded up the young fieldhands coming off the south forty. "I'm giving each of you a chance you'll never get again," he said to the group of dark-skinned young men in ragged clothes. "We're at war with Pennsylvania, as you all know. Any of you who volunteers to fight, will terminate his obligation to this estate."

"Are you saying we'll be free, sir?" one of the young men asked.

"That's right," Master Easley said.

Every hand in the group rose into the air, along with a chorus of "I'll go!"

"Now, I can only take ten of you," the master said. "We can't spare you all. There's still a lot of work to be done bringing in this year's crop."

Eustace pressed forward, trying to catch the master's eye. He was not the biggest or the strongest among the other fieldhands and was worried he'd be passed over. To Eustace's surprise, he was the third one chosen.

Ten young men from the Easley plantation left the next morning, under the eye of an overseer, for a mustering camp in Charlottesville.

Two weeks later, Eustace was in a muddy field near Brandy Station, Virginia. Wearing a gray tunic with a matching cap and armed only with a pitchfork, he stood in formation before the front lines of the invading army from Pennsylvania. Lined up alongside Eustace were several hundred other negro troops, similarly armed. Behind them, in a separate unit, were white regulars with muskets.

From his horse, their white commander said, "You're going to attack those pennies or you'll die," he said, pointing toward the enemy lines. "If we see your black faces running back this way, you'll be shot."

When the order came to charge, Eustace clutched his pitchfork and ran toward the enemy. A moving target would be harder to hit, he told himself.

A cloud of smoke rose from the Pennsylvania lines as over a hundred muskets fired. Eustace could hear the hiss of bullets and the wet, sickening sound of lead striking the flesh of the men around him. Praying, he charged ahead, grateful for the cloud of smoke from the enemy guns. The pennies were now shooting blind.

Screams of pain rose as more of his comrades were struck. Still, he continued forward, certain that retreat would be worse. The enemy lines were still a hundred paces ahead.

Then, he heard a bugle call and looked behind him. Virginia's white troops were moving forward. Certain he would be caught in a crossfire, Eustace dropped to the ground, pretending to be wounded.

The decision saved him.

When the white Virginians reached him, Eustace rose and charged alongside them. Reaching the enemy lines, his pitchfork became a useful weapon. The fighting would now be hand-to-hand.

The savagery that followed still haunted him.

After the battle, the body count showed two-thirds of the negro troops had died trying to reach the Pennsylvania lines. The dead included five of the young men from Eustace's plantation.

Four days later, Eustace's unit was again deployed using the pitchfork assault near the town of Winchester. Eustace repeated his charge-and-drop tactic and survived. His unit, however, was reduced to twenty percent of their original strength.

What was left of Eustace's battalion was merged into another negro regiment as General Robert E. Lee began marching north. After three days, Eustace's column forded the widest river he had ever seen.

"What's this river called?" Eustace asked his negro sergeant as they waded through the waist-deep water.

"This is the Potomac, son. We're marching into Pennsylvania."

At camp that night, there were whispers among the troops in his regiment.

"They're using us for cannon fodder," one of the older soldiers said. "It's only a matter of time. None of us are coming out of this alive."

"I am," another veteran said. "When the time is right, I'm high tailing it. They don't have slave catchers up here in Pennsylvania. And they say some folks will help you get away."

"I heard that, too," another soldier said. "They're called Quakers. They say those folks are absolitionists."

"Abolitionists," the veteran corrected him. "They live in a city called Philadelphia. I aim to get there."

Eustace listened quietly. There was no honor in this duty. His only hope was to stay alive until he could find a way out. That opportunity came five days later in a town called Gettysburg.

The pennies were dug in on Cemetery Ridge, a stretch of high ground overlooking the town. Eustace's negro unit had been attached to a general named Pickett who General Lee had chosen to take Cemetery Ridge.

The news worried Eustace. Pickett was known to hang deserters.

Lined up alongside white units this time but still armed with a pitchfork, Eustace looked toward the enemy lines.

At Brandy Station and Winchester, they'd charged across a few hundred yards. Here, the enemy was nearly a mile away over open terrain. To make matters worse, they'd need to climb a steep rise at the end to reach the Pennsylvania lines.

For nearly an hour, the Virginians waited to attack in neat regimental rows. A blistering July sun beat down on them.

Then the artillery barrage began.

Eustace stood at attention, trembling with fear as a torrent of shells exploded around him. Some men vanished in a black cloud, others were shattered, their limbs flying. Through it all, the living never broke ranks.

By the time the order to advance came, Pickett had

lost nearly half his troops. Pitchfork in hand, Eustace started toward the enemy as the shells continued to rain on them. When men around him fell, Eustace rushed ahead to close ranks. He was terrified yet determined. If the white troops could endure this, he would as well.

For the next half-hour, Eustace marched in formation as withering volleys of musket fire joined the artillery in mowing down their ranks. The men kept marching, looking side to side to see how many were left. Eustace had no doubt the attack would fail now. Only one question remained. How many of them would die before they were ordered to retreat?

The order never came. But, as if moving with a single mind, the lines broke and the men began falling back – a few steps at first, then finally at a run.

Eustace was surprised how fast his legs had carried him as he reached Virginia's lines. There, he found all order gone.

Medics tended to the rows of wounded screaming for help or groaning in pain. The lucky few not hurt wandered in confusion, their commanders dead or missing.

The road to their headquarters was a logjam as ambulances tried to ferry the wounded away and ammunition wagons tried to reach the front.

Dazed, Eustace followed the road for a while, lost in the stream of soldiers. Near a copse of trees, he walked into the bushes and shed his army tunic and cap. By nightfall, he was miles away from Gettysburg.

Eight days later, he wandered into Philadelphia's 7th Ward. Eustace was not alone. The streets of the city's negro district were filled with new arrivals from the south. Churches, civic groups and many local families provided meals, shelter and help finding work for the tide of exiles from slavery.

Eustace's new life in the city began mucking stables. After a time, he became an apprentice blacksmith.

Attending services at Mother Bethel church, he met Alice. She was a runaway from South Carolina. Their courtship was brief. They both wanted a family more than anything else.

Now, Alice had borne his first child, a boy they called James. And that's why Eustace had a bible under his arm.

Walking into Mother Bethel church, Eustace found the minister sweeping the choir loft. Holding out the brand-new bible, Eustace said, "Reverend, would you write something in this bible for me?"

"Of course, Eustace," he said, putting down the broom. "Let's go to the church office." Behind his desk, with pen in hand, the minister said, "What would you like me to write?"

"My son was born yesterday. Alice and me, we named him James Harold Easley. Could you write his name and the day he was born here?" he said, pointing to the bible's inside cover."

"I'd be honored to do that, Eustace."

"And leave plenty of room on that page, reverend," Eustace said. "That bible is going to be handed down to a family of free men and women for a long, long time."

Six generations later, the inscriptions would include the Director of the Security Bureau in the People's Republic of Pennsylvania, James William Easley.

~=~

| Day Seven |

VANNES, FRANCIA

General Regis Lafoy stood before the large portrait of the prime minister on the wall of his office. Inspecting his reflection in the glass-covered photo, Lafoy straightened the rows of service ribbons on his dress tunic.

Wearing a ceremonial uniform for a video conference was rare. But Lafoy wanted to pull out all the stops for his meeting at 1000 hours with the chair of the military appropriations committee. Snagging the funds to arm his regiment with the coveted new Berthier tanks would punch his ticket to another star. His allies within the PM's party had assured him of that.

Following a knock on the door, his adjutant stepped into the smartly decorated office and saluted. "There's a call for you, sir."

"Sergeant, you know I have less than ten minutes before a conference with Paris. This damned well better be important or you'll be digging latrines in Guiana next week."

"I have the aide for a nic general on the line, sir. She says it's urgent her commander speaks to you. The general's name is Matthew Drake with the Virginia Ordnance Corps."

"Tell him I'm busy."

"Sir, the aide said it was important. She said if you don't answer, the next call you get will be from Helen Levet."

"All right. Put him through," he said, waving the soldier out of his office. The general then walked behind his desk and sat down.

When the phone buzzed, Lafoy pressed the speaker button and said, "What can I do for you, General?"

"Stand by for General Drake please," a female voice said.

Lafoy's face reddened. This insolent nic was violating military protocol by having his aide make a superior officer wait on the line.

A male voice with a thick Britannic accent came from the speaker. "General Lafoy, this is urgent, so I'll keep my call brief," he said. "There's been a serious problem in the shipment of a certain type of ordnance your regiment delivered to our facility in Charlottesville. I trust you understand what I'm referring to."

"I know about the shipment, but I don't know why you're involved." Levet had told him nothing about this General Drake.

"As we both know, General, this ordnance is highly classified. I've been assigned by Paris to monitor security – and I've just learned there's been a mix up in the shipment. Some of the ordnance you sent is C4. Three kilos, to be exact," Drake said.

Shit, thought Lafoy. Mistaking C4 for bloom could make its first tactical use by the nics a failure – and that would reflect poorly on *him*. "Thank you for bringing that to my attention. I'll make sure the officer responsible is severely punished," Lafoy said. He'd wring the nuts off the shave tail he'd recruited to package the bloom.

"That's not enough," the nic said. "Out of respect for a fellow soldier, I'm going to give you a choice, General. Will you tell Helen Levet about this foul-up or should I do it?"

Lafoy's mouth went dry. Levet had the ear of the prime minister. Without the right spin, this could wreck his career. "I'll inform her," Lafoy said. "You have my word as a soldier."

After ending the call, Lafoy muttered to himself. "I'll keep my word, you impudent nic. But there's no reason I have to hurry."

PARIS, FRANCIA

Standing near the hotel room window, Brody and Olivia were huddled close, listening to Lafoy's voice over the mobile phone's speaker.

"I'll inform her. You have my word as a soldier," Lafoy said before ending the call.

Brody tapped the microphone icon on his phone and stopped recording the conversation.

"Yes!" Olivia said, clenching her fist in triumph. "It was Helen Levet — I knew it!"

"Your idea was brilliant, Olivia," he said with a broad smile." I doubt Lafoy will ever call Levet."

"Even if he does, it won't matter. We nabbed them both," she said, then walked to the mini bar. "This calls for a celebration. Cognac again?"

"That sounds good," he said. "But I'll need to call my boss first."

"Of course," she said. "I'll go for a walk."

"Stay," he said, dialing the phone. "You're on the inside now." He kept the call off speaker, though. There was no point in revealing anything to her about Jim Easley.

Carrying singles of Pernod and cognac from the mini bar, Olivia sat down on the bed. Opening the Pernod, she took a long pull as Brody dialed the phone.

"I've got it, boss. The whole chain," Brody said after Jim Easley answered. "Lafoy got his orders to ship the bloom from Helen Levet. She's the prime minister's national security adviser."

"Are you sure?"

"I called Lafoy posing as a cherry general and he confirmed the connection," Brody said. "I'll send you a recording of the whole conversation."

"Son, you have brass balls," Easley said chuckling. "Did the data our team sent on Lafoy help?"

"I never got it."

"Then how in the hell did you figure this out?"

"A very reliable source – but one that's going to stay confidential," Brody said, then looked at Olivia and smiled.

"I understand that. But Le Figaro is going to ask for a source before they'll run the story."

"Tell them to call Lafoy," Brody said. "He'll throw Levet under the bus. The guy is a worm."

"I have to admit, stories have been written on a lot less than we already have," Easley said. "I'll advise the premier to put the Charlottesville strike on hold. Good work, son."

"Thanks, boss."

"One more thing," Easley said. "I don't want to hear from you for at least a week. You earned the rest," he said, then ended the call.

After forwarding the recording of LaFoy's call to his boss, Brody exhaled slowly. "You may have stopped a war, Olivia."

"What do you mean?"

"I can't tell you more. But believe me. Leaking this story to the media will save lives – on both sides of our border."

"Then let's drink to that," she said, handing him the cognac.

***

When I handed Hassan the cognac bottle, he tapped it against my single of Pernod. "À nos amours," he said, meeting my eyes.

Gazes locked, we both downed a long swallow.

"Interesting toast," I said, swirling my bottle. "What *are* your loves?"

Hassan turned his eyes toward the ceiling, then back to me. "Mostly this, I guess."

"You love being a spy?"

"I love feeling alive."

I nodded. "I can understand that," I said. The sting on Lafoy had been a thrill that awakened something dormant — and left me craving more.

Hassan reached into his jacket. "Smoke?" he asked, offering an open pack of Admirals.

"Thanks," I said, taking a cigarette.

Flipping back the cap on his zippo, Hassan struck a flame and held it out.

I leaned close to him, my pulse racing. Then, instead of lighting my Admiral, I tossed the cigarette aside and blew out the lighter's flame. Looking into his eyes, I pulled Hassan against me.

Hassan dropped the lighter, cradled my face and kissed me.

He brushed his lips gently over mine at first, pausing to let me respond. My passion stirring, I parted my lips, welcoming a deeper kiss. Hassan obliged.

Body tingling, I embraced him, feeling the taut muscles of his back. He responded by caressing my waist, hands slowly moving up until they reached my breasts.

My breath growing ragged, I pulled him down onto the bed.

We shed our clothes, exploring each other's bodies. The long months of abstinence fired my passion. After Hassan put on a sheath from the amenity kit by the bed, I lost track of time until we were finally spent.

With my head against his chest, we both fell asleep.

After a time, a knock on the door awakened us. "Housekeeping," a woman's voice said from the hallway.

"Maybe it's time we checked out," Hassan said, rubbing his eyes.

I touched his arm and whispered, "Do you have any place to go today?"

Hassan shook his head.

I called out toward the door. "No housekeeping today. Thank you." I then turned to Hassan and kissed him. "If you're not going anywhere, mister, we're just getting started."

***

Astride a bicycle, wearing a helmet and a yellow courier's vest, Bernard approached the five-story apartment building overlooking the entrance to Parc Poyet. After parking his bike, Bernard entered the building's vestibule and pressed the button above mailbox 404.

A familiar voice came from the wall speaker. "Who is this?" Ludolph Eltz asked.

"Good day, sir. I'm with LeJour Express," Bernard said, using a thick Marseille accent. "I have a document for Monsieur Ludolph Eltz that needs a signature of receipt," he said. "Is he home?"

"Who is it from?"

"Frederick Fullenkamp," Bernard replied. He was certain that

Eltz would ask about the source of the document. So he'd given him the name of the Freedom Coalition's chairman.

A short buzz from the speaker was followed by the click of a bolt as Eltz unlocked the main door to the apartments. "Bring up the document," he said.

Bernard passed into the lobby, pressed the elevator button and stepped inside.

He should have been angry. But in truth, Bernard was enjoying the chance to pose as a courier. Some of his contract work involved role playing. Bernard loved those jobs the most. It was real-world acting experience he hoped to use in films someday.

Finding where Eltz lived had not been difficult. Bernard had low friends in high places. Now, he'd have the chance to rough up Eltz a little. Nothing major. Just a shiner and some bruises, maybe a broken arm. That would send a message to everyone in *le milieu*: Make a chump out of *Le Fleurist* and you'll pay a price.

At the door of apartment 404, Bernard rang the doorbell and waited. Eltz had never seen him. So his face would not spook the German.

Eltz opened the door halfway. Peering into the hallway, he extended his hand. "I'll take the document and sign it. You wait here."

Instead of handing him the envelope, Bernard shoved hard against the door, slamming it into Eltz's face. The blow sent the German reeling to the floor.

Stepping into the apartment's living room, Bernard closed the door behind him. "You almost got me killed, motherfucker," he growled.

Rubbing his swelling brow, Eltz said, "I don't know what you're talking about."

"You don't, huh? I'm *Le Fleurist*."

Eltz's eyes widened. "Whatever happened, I can assure you it was never my intent to put you in danger."

"I walked into an ambush at your dead drop. Whether it was intentional or just plain stupid doesn't matter. You made me look bad. Now you're going to pay for it."

Eltz rose to his knees and pressed his palms together. "Please... Don't kill me. I'll pay you double – even if the job's not done," he said, voice quivering.

Bernard mulled over the offer. He'd take Eltz's money and still rough him up for good measure – if he wasn't lying. "Do you have the money here?"

"Yes, yes," Eltz said, rising to his feet. "The money is in my study. Let me get it," he said, walking through a doorway off the living room.

Bernard followed Eltz into a wood paneled room.

"I have the money right here," Eltz said, then walked behind the desk and opened a drawer.

Bernard's mouth gaped as Eltz took a pistol from the drawer and fired.

Aimed from the hip, the German's shot missed him.

As Eltz raised the weapon to eye level, preparing to fire again, Bernard dropped to the floor behind the desk. Drawing his pistol as he rolled to the right, Bernard rose to one knee and fired twice. The 9mm slugs struck Eltz in the chest, knocking him against the wall.

His eyes still open, Eltz slid down the wall, leaving a smear of blood on the wood paneling.

Bernard rose to his feet and put away his gun. "Shit," he

muttered. This caper hadn't gone as he'd intended. There was only one thing to do now: make this look like a robbery.

Fortunately, he'd done that many times before.

1933

PHILADELPHIA, PENNSYLVANIA

The plainclothes guards escorted a short man with a pencil mustache up the carpeted staircase at the presidential residence. When they reached the double doors on the second floor, one of the guards opened them and said, "The premier is expecting you."

Inside the opulent office, the tall and swarthy figure of Morris Santee Cooper waved the visitor inside. "It's good to see you, Rick," he said as the guards closed the doors, leaving them alone.

"Can I still call you Mo?" Rick asked, walking toward Cooper and shaking his hand.

"Yeah, but just when we're alone," Cooper said. "You understand why, right?"

"Sure. I get it, Mo. But what I don't get is why you asked the barber from your old neighborhood to come here. They just made you the premier of Pennsylvania."

"The People's Republic of Pennsylvania," Cooper corrected him with a smirk.

Rick grinned back at him. "Right. So why the hell am I here?"

"To cut my hair," Cooper said, waving toward a side table with an array of combs, scissors, cape and an electric hair clipper.

"You're kidding, right? You can get the best barbers in Philly up here."

"Nobody's ever cut my hair like you do, Rick," Cooper said, sitting down in a chair near the table. "Why don't you get started?"

"Same as always?" Rick asked, placing the cape over the premier's shoulders.

"Sure," Cooper said.

The premier was silent as the barber began working with a comb and scissors. But when he turned on the electric clippers, Cooper looked at Rick, then touched his ear and waved his finger around the room.

Rick nodded, getting the message. The room was bugged.

Standing up, Cooper moved closer to the barber and spoke softly. "Look, Rick. Everyone around me is a stranger. I need people who knew me before all this crazy business happened. I need somebody I can trust."

Rick placed the clippers on the table, still buzzing. "I kept up with you in the papers. They started calling you the People's Hero when you went to jail for refusing your colonel's orders to shoot the strikers. What I can't figure is how you got the rest of the Army to mutiny from prison."

After months of strikes and riots over low pay and hunger, President Norville Perry had declared martial law and deployed Army units to every major city in

Pennsylvania.

"I didn't have anything to do with the mutiny against the officers. The other sergeants and enlisted men did that on their own while I was in jail.

"The papers said the mutiny made Perry go into exile. He didn't have the army to do his dirty work anymore."

President Perry, a Constitutionalist serving his third term, had fled across the western border and sought asylum from the governor of New Francia.

"Didn't surprise me he turned tail," Cooper said. "Perry was a coward and a crook."

"What I can't figure is why the People's Party chose an army master sergeant to be the new premier."

"They used me to take control of the troops."

"I don't get you."

"I was grateful when the Party people got me out of jail. But they had a condition. I had to convince the sergeants who became the army's leaders to meet with the Party," Cooper said. "These guys trusted me. I was one of them. So they agreed." Cooper's voice grew hoarse. "There were fourteen of them. The Party people sent limousines and brought them to a mansion in the country, fed them and got them liquored up. Then they threw them all in jail on corruption charges."

Rick's mouth gaped.

"The Party planned it well," Cooper continued. "Next day, new officers show up at the bases replacing my old friends. The Party's going to take good care of you these guys tell the troops. New uniforms, better food and housing. Then they start cutting paychecks. More money than these soldiers have ever seen. It worked. The troops forgot about my comrades. And the Party had the army in its pocket.

"Mo, that's unbelievable."

"I know. The Party was counting on that."

"How come they didn't get rid of you, too?"

"I'm still useful to them – for now," Cooper said. "The leaders of the Party are smart people, Rick ... union bosses, politicians, professors, students. But all of them want to be in charge now that Perry's gone," he explained. "So they picked me to be premier. The Party leaders think I'm a dumb, jerkwater soldier who isn't on to their game. But they all want to keep me around cause I'll be easy to replace once the big shots fight it out."

Rick rubbed his mustache. "Have you thought about resigning?"

"I don't think that would be good for my health."

"Why not call on some of your other friends in the army for help?"

"The bodyguards who brought you here have orders from the Party. No visitors without their permission. Anybody military is off the guest list."

"I guess they didn't see me as much of a threat."

"That's true," Cooper said. "But don't sell yourself short."

"What do you mean?"

"I need you to get a message to someone in Francia's embassy."

Rick tugged at his collar. "I don't know, Mo. That's a high-toned crowd over there. I'd really stand out."

"You can do this, Rick. I got a note here," he said, handing him an envelope from his pocket. "Tell them it's from the premier of Pennsylvania and you want to give the message to the ambassador himself."

"Is this some kind of treason?"

Cooper scoffed. "Hell no, Rick. Things are going

to get cockeyed here when the Party tries to replace me. I want to have enough francs to straighten things out," he said. "It might save my life. Will you help me?"

"Sure, Mo."

"Good. I'll send for you again next week. That should give you enough time to pick up the cash," Cooper said, then turned off the clippers. "That looks great, Rick. Can you come back next week?"

"Yes," Rick said. "I can do that."

Cooper walked to the door and opened it. "Thanks, Rick. I'll be in touch," he said before the barber left.

Returning to his desk, Cooper looked over his agenda. All of it was fluff. Speeches at schools, tours of factories, meetings with farmers. He was the face of the People's Party of Pennsylvania. But the brains behind the party was a rat's nest of intrigue and double dealing.

Cooper had no doubt that Pennsylvania was better off without Norville Perry as its president. In fact, there hadn't been a horse whisker's difference between Pennsylvania's political parties for as long as he could remember.

Both the Constitutionalists and the Republicans tried their damnedest to get richer whenever they got their hands on the reins. Everyone knew both parties manipulated districts and vote counts to rig the elections. The winners weren't the best candidates. They were the best cheaters.

In the end, though, they were all Francia's lackeys. The toads controlled all the major industries. He knew that firsthand.

He'd been born in a mining town run by Garnier Coal. Like all the other miners, his family lived in a company shack. They bought their food and clothes at the company store. His father had died from black lung, his brother in a mining accident. After his mother died of pneumonia, Morris walked 28 miles to Pottsville and enlisted.

At eighteen, he'd learned a hard lesson about his country. The only place a Pennsylvanian could get ahead was through the government. Of course, that explained why officials in both parties had become so corrupt.

But was this new one-party system any better?

There was one thing in its favor: The Party got things done.

Since taking power four months ago, the People's Party of Pennsylvania had abolished the constitution that included the presidency and the General Assembly. In its place, all government decisions would be made by the Party's Central Committee.

Many of the top committee members had been smitten by the newsreels coming out of Soviet Russia. Their one-party system had created a worker's paradise over there. So they figured that would work here, too.

The committee's first directives had been to root out Perry's loyalists in the government. Hundreds of them were jailed. Now, the members of the committee were busy turning on each other. Cooper was sure that, before long, they'd turn on him, too.

If they stayed in power.

There was talk in the committee of nationalizing major industries. If that happened, Francia would bring down the hammer. The Party's only recourse would be an alliance with the Soviets. Trading one master for another did not seem like a good bargain to Cooper – no matter what the Soviet newsreels claimed.

That's why he'd reached out to the toads for help. The devil you knew was better than the devil you didn't

Cooper sighed, opened a desk drawer and brought out a fifth of rye. As he took a long pull from the bottle, the door opened.

The Head of Security entered the room, followed by two bodyguards. Between the agents was Rick, his face bloodied and bruised.

"Morris Santee Cooper," the security chief said. "I'm placing you under arrest for corruption and conspiring against the people of Pennsylvania," he then pointed to Rick. "This man's testimony and the message you gave him will prove that."

Rick grimaced and said, "Sorry, Mo."

Cooper shook his head. "I don't blame you, Rick. I got you into this mess."

The first premier of Pennsylvania was tried and sentenced to life in prison six days later.

Historians would call him Morris of the Hundred Days.

***

That same day, in the port of Philadelphia, the crew of the SS Kingston had almost finished unloading her cargo.

"Bring up that load of coffee, Sean," the bosun yelled from the deck down into the ship's hold.

Following the bosun's order, Lin Xiáng Ying hooked the crane line to a skid of bundled coffee sacks and watched the dockside derrick lift it out. Wiping his brow, Xiáng looked around the hold and smiled. The compartment was nearly empty. His wages and a shore leave were not far away.

Educated by British missionaries, Xiáng had joined
the Kingston's crew in Canton after they'd lost a
deckhand to scurvy. When the captain asked his name,
he'd said "Xiáng." To the captain, the name sounded
like Sean. So Sean he became.

Leaving Canton, the Kingston had followed the
Asian coast north, docking in the Soviet province of
Alyaska. The city of Kodiak was very different from
China. The people spoke Russian, the buildings had
straight roofs, and the canning factories near the port
reeked of fish.

Crossing the Aleutian Straights, they followed
the North American coast south and docked in San
Francisco. Xiáng heard Spanish for the first time in
the Mexican city with the largest bay he'd ever seen.
At the rest of the ports around the horn, the locals
spoke Spanish or French. It was not until Savannah
and Richmond, their last two ports of call, that Xiáng
heard English spoken.

Arriving at the port of Philadelphia a day earlier,
Xiáng had noticed the abandoned wharves along
the Delaware River. The dockside warehouses were
covered in hand-painted slogans and posters for causes
he did not understand.

"All crew on deck!" the bosun yelled after they'd
finished unloading the Kingston.

The thirty-two-man crew gathered on the main
deck. Standing near the edge of the group, Xiáng
noticed something alarming.

On the dock below, over a dozen policemen
carrying truncheons were approaching the Kingston
led by a man in a black suit.

Without asking for permission to board, the
stranger walked up the gangplank, the policemen
behind him. Once on deck, the policemen surrounded

the crew. Stepping onto the forecastle, the man in the suit addressed the sailors.

"This vessel is in arrears and is now the property of the Banque de Francia," he said in English with a French burr. "You will be escorted to your quarters to remove your personal possessions. Any resistance will be dealt with harshly and will earn you a one-year jail sentence."

"We're due our pay!" one of the men called out.

"Your wages were the responsibility of the former owners," the black suit said. "They are in default and have no money to pay you."

Angry and confused, the crew did not move.

Then, the bosun said, "You heard the man, lads. Get on about it or these coppers are going to crack some heads and you'll be leaving with empty pockets all the same."

A half-hour later all the crewmen were on the dock, their possessions crammed into duffel bags. Xiáng followed the others as they wandered off the quay.

"You think them jailing their premier had anything to do with our getting sacked?" the radio man asked.

"I know fuck all about what's happening in this dump," a young redhead muttered.

"I'm getting me a berth on another ship in port," said an older sailor.

"Good luck with that, codger," the redhead said. "Nobody's hiring. The lefties around here keep starting riots and strikes. It's killing the shipping business."

A deckhand named Cutter sidled next to Xiáng. "They got a Chinatown here, Sean," he said. "You thinking of going there?"

Xiáng shrugged. "I do not know where to go."

"It's not far. I've been in Philadelphia before," Cutter said. "C'mon, I'll show you the way."

"What will you do for work here?" Xiáng asked as they walked.

"My cards will always keep me fed, boyo," Cutter said.

Xiáng knew Cutter was not boasting. Aboard the Kingston, Xiáng had seen him play a game with three cards he called Find the Lady. "If cards can make you money. Why do you work on a ship?"

"In the card trade, you need to keep moving – unless you have powerful friends."

Their walk had brought them to the corner of Race and Vine streets. In both directions, Xiáng saw shops and restaurants with signs in Chinese characters.

"Why have you brought me here?" Xiáng asked.

"I figure you might introduce me to some of the right people."

"I do not know anyone here, Cutter."

"No, but I think you might open some doors I can't."

"What do you mean?"

"I want you to vouch for me with the tong bosses," Cutter said. "I can't set up a game without their permission."

Xiáng knew the tong well from Canton. He shook his head. "I will not do this, Cutter."

"I'll give you part of the take, Sean – and I'll cut the tong bosses in, too."

"No. The tong only bring trouble."

"C'mon, mate. I brought you here, didn't I?"

"You don't need me to find the tong, Cutter. Start your game on the street here. They will find you. Promise them money and they will let you stay," Xiáng said, then walked away.

A few blocks down the street, Xiáng saw a small sign in the window of the Lee Fong Laundry. Written in Chinese characters, the sign said: Worker wanted. By the end of the day, Xiáng had a job and a small room in a boarding house nearby.

Along with washing and ironing, Xiáng made deliveries to Lee Fong's wealthier clients. On a delivery to a mansion in Society Hill, Xiáng met Sarah Wilson. She worked there as a day maid and managed the incoming and outgoing laundry.

It was Sarah's bronze skin and honey-colored eyes that caught his attention. But it was the kindness of the nineteen-year-old that won his heart. Unlike many other servants in rich homes, Sarah treated him with courtesy, offering him a pleasant greeting and water in the summer or coffee in the winter.

After nearly a year, Xiáng mustered the nerve to reveal his intentions.

"You always keep beautiful flowers in the kitchen, Sarah," he said, putting down a large bundle of clothes on a counter. "The flowers are also beautiful in Fairmount Park. Would you join me there on Sunday?"

Sarah looked into his eyes, then turned away and smiled. "Yes, Sean. I'd like that."

They'd agreed to meet at noon, but Xiáng arrived at the park a half-hour early. He wanted to claim the bench with the best view of the gardens in the park. Despite the turmoil in the gweilo world, the park in Chinatown was busy.

To his delight, Sarah was already at the park. But he found her on a secluded bench away from the popular plots of flowers. She wore a hat with a veil that hid her golden eyes.

"Would you like to walk and see the flowers?" he

asked, standing before her.

"Let's sit here and talk," she said, tapping the far side of the bench. "I've wondered why you came here from China, but I was too embarrassed to ask."

"My parents are poor farmers. They were happy when I entered the missionary school in Canton and learned to speak English. That helped me find a berth on an English merchant ship."

"Have you traveled very far? I've always dreamed of that."

"The city a sailor sees is not pretty. But the beauty of the sea is like nothing else," he said. "In Alyaska, the floating mountains of ice are many shades of green and blue. And the mountains of South America have jungles at their feet and snow on their peaks," he said. "The nights on the ocean may be the best of all. Under the moon, the water is like a black jewel."

"You've been to all these places, why did you decide to stay in Philadelphia?"

"The owners of our ship ran out of money. They sold everything and left the crew here."

"Do you want to go back to China?" she asked.

He looked at her for a long moment. "Not anymore."

"I'm very glad to hear that," she said smiling.

Their meeting in the park became the first of many over the next few months. At times, they were bold enough to hold each other's hands as they spoke.

Xiáng learned that Sarah's family had been in Philadelphia for three generations. Her grandfather had been a freeman who took a Quaker wife. Her father was a tanner who owned a business along the river with his three sons.

Xiáng and Sarah's happy times together ended in March.

As he entered the kitchen with a package of laundry, Sarah began to cry. "I can't see you anymore when we're not at work," she said, wiping her eyes.

Xiáng's heart sank. "Why not?"

"Please don't ask. I'm too ashamed to tell you."

"What could be so shameful?"

Sarah lowered her eyes. "One of my brothers saw us together and told my father. Daddy says we can't keep company anymore."

Crushed, Xiáng returned to work. More bad news waited there.

Lee Fong stood by the door, a scowl darkening his face. "I heard what's happening," he said in Cantonese. "You will stop consorting with that woman. It's bad for business. My wife will be delivering the laundry there from now on."

Lying in bed at his rooming house that night, Xiáng stared at the ceiling.

Sarah's father and Lee Fong were wrong. If Sarah would have him, he would be a good husband and father to their children. There had to be some way to convince these men.

The following day, Xiáng left the laundry for his afternoon deliveries. As he turned onto a quiet side street, three young men approached him. They all had Sarah's shade of skin.

"Are you Sean?" the largest of them asked.

Xiáng nodded. "I am."

Grabbing the edge of his cart, the young men turned it over onto the street, sending his laundry bundles flying. Then, the largest one grabbed Xiáng by the collar.

"Our sister doesn't need a Fu Manchu for a boyfriend. Get it?" he said, shoving Xiáng in the chest.

"You tell him, William!" one of his brothers shouted.

"I have a job. I can provide for Sarah," Xiáng said calmly.

"Are you deaf, boy?" he said, then shoved Xiáng to the pavement this time.

Rising to his feet, Xiáng said, "I love your sister, William. She will be well treated—"

William punched Xiáng in the gut. He crumpled to the ground, gasping for breath.

Pointing a finger in Xiáng's face, he yelled, "You get up again and it will be the last time you ever walk! Stay away from our sister!"

As Xiáng held his belly, the four young men left.

Watching the scuffle from the corner was Xiáng's old crewmate, Cutter.

When Xiáng arrived for work the next morning at dawn, Lee Fong pulled him aside. "You've stirred up a lot of trouble, fool. The tong got wind that you were roughed up yesterday. Now they're planning revenge against the men who beat you."

"How did the tong find out?"

"The gweilo you worked with on the ship saw it. He cheats on cards for the tong on the street."

"Why would the tong care about me?"

"You're Chinese, and the beating happened on their territory. To accept that from the heirén without revenge would be a serious loss of face."

"Do you know when the tong will move against them?"

"Stay out of this, Xiáng. They've started already. You can't stop them."

Xiáng turned and headed for the door. "I'm sorry, sir. I will not be working today."

On the sidewalk, he broke into a run toward the

Wilson Tannery near the river. It was the only place the tong could be sure of finding Sarah's brothers.

A block from the tannery, Xiáng saw the tong's men. They'd set a trap. One of them stood on the corner as a lookout. Five more waited, out of sight in an alley. Looking down the cross street, Xiáng saw William. He was two blocks away and walking toward their trap.

Xiáng approached the men in the alley.

"I know what you gentlemen are here to do," Xiáng said in Cantonese. "Please stop. My name is Lin Xiáng Ying. I'm the offended party and I absolve you of defending my honor."

"That may be so, Xiáng Ying," the tong leader said. "But honor cannot be satisfied unless the offender apologizes."

"One of the brothers you pursue is coming now. I can get an apology if you'll let me talk to him."

"You have five minutes," their leader said.

Walking quickly, Xiáng rounded the corner. William was ten paces from the hidden trap.

"Boy, you here for me to beat on you again?" William said, his eyes narrowing.

"I am not here for a beating, William. I am here to spare you from one. Six members of the Chinese tong are waiting for you around the corner. They will avenge your actions against me."

William scoffed. "Really? That's funny, little man."

"After they beat you, they will burn your family's business to the ground."

"Let them try."

"They will succeed. If not today, another time. These men are professionals, William. You are putting your family's future at risk over a matter of pride. But the tannery does not have to burn. I can show you how to stop it."

"I'm not apologizing."

"Under Chinese customs, that is not necessary."

"What do you mean?"

At that moment, the six tong members stepped out of the alley. William's eyes widened.

Xiáng stepped close to William and spoke softly. "You will say one word to these men, and then nod your head."

"What do I say?"

"Dway-boo-chee."

"What does that mean?"

"It means you wish peace with honor."

"You mean a truce?"

"That is a good translation. Are you prepared?"

William nodded.

Xiáng then walked to the tong leader and spoke in Cantonese. "This man is ready to show contrition, sir."

"We can forget this unpleasantness if honor is observed," the tong leader said.

Xiáng waved for William to come forward.

"Dway-boo-chee," William said, then nodded.

The tong leader bowed to Xiáng. "You understand our customs and have conducted this matter well, Lin Xiáng Ying. You will always have our respect and protection."

The men of the tong then walked away.

William held out his palm. "You took a risk doing this, Sean," he said. "Thank you."

"Shaking his hand, Xiáng said, "I love your sister, William. I would do anything to protect her – and her family."

"I'll tell my father what you did here. He might change his mind about you."

As William walked toward the tannery, Xiáng felt a pang of regret. The tong was never going to burn down the Wilson's business. But William would have never agreed to an apology on the threat of a beating alone. A lie was like a blade. It could be used to hurt or to heal.

Things changed when news of Xiáng's deed spread. Lee Fong allowed him to deliver laundry to Sarah again. There, he learned her family would no longer oppose their acquaintance.

During a meeting in the park several months later, they sat side by side on a bench. Xiáng dropped to a knee beside her.

"In Canton, a man's family proposes with many gifts to the woman's family. But we are not in China," he said, then pulled a gold ring from his pocket and took her hand. "This is the correct custom, yes?"

"Yes. That's the right custom. But I can't marry you, Sean," she said, drawing her hand away. "My family has accepted you. But most folks around here would not approve. We'd never be happy with so much hate around."

"Do you love me?"

She nodded. "I do. Very much."

"I love you, Sarah. Let our love be stronger than the hate."

After a moment, Sarah held out her hand.

Later that year, they were married at the Fellowship House Church. Sarah's family and Lee Fong's relatives joined them at the ceremony.

Fifty-two years later, Sarah buried her husband and died three years after him. Both funerals were attended by seven children, their spouses, and eleven grandchildren.

One of those granddaughters would give birth to a child she named Brody.

| DAY EIGHT |

PARIS, FRANCIA

The dawn was glowing through the hotel room window when I opened my eyes. Hassan's breath was warm on my shoulder as he cradled my waist, still asleep. Relishing the softness of the pillow against my cheek, I basked in the moment. We'd slept for over ten hours, an absolute extravagance.

The last time I'd felt like this was on my honeymoon. Dan and I had reveled in a marathon of sex at a Blue Ridge resort. That feast of pleasure had marked the beginning of my new life as a wife. But my days as Mrs. Dan Syme had barely lasted a year. I had no idea that being married to an army officer would relegate me to the circle of wives on the base – even though I was an officer as well. The wives' world of babies, bargains and base gossip was more than I could stand.

In any case, this time with Hassan was hardly a honeymoon.

He would soon be gone, and my new life would begin – alone

and on the run.

I'd never forget this time with Hassan, though. I was sure of that.

Hassan stirred and I turned to face him. When he opened his eyes, I sat up and said, "It's time for me to go."

"What's your hurry?" he asked, taking my hand.

"I need to get out of Francia."

Hassan shook his head. "The SS has sent your name and photo to every border post in Francia by now, Olivia. You need to lay low until things cool off."

I chewed my lip. He was right. But my pride wouldn't let me admit the obvious: After I paid for the identity documents, train fare to the border, and some new clothes, I would not have enough money to extend my stay in Paris. "I should go," I finally said, rising from the bed.

Hassan pulled me back. "Look, I know you need more money. I can help you stay here longer."

"Why would you do that? You got what you wanted. Your boss knows who's behind the bloom pipeline."

Hassan stroked my hair. "This isn't about my mission. I'm enjoying our time together."

"I am too," I said. "But where does that leave *us*?"

"I've got nothing on my plate for a while. Beyond that, I don't know," he said. "Is that enough for you?"

I'd never lived like this before, moment to moment. It was terrifying – and thrilling. "Know any good places for breakfast?" I asked, smoothing the hair along his temple.

"Let's stay in and order room service," he said, then reached for the TV remote on the nightstand. "Our story may have hit the news channels."

By the time our breakfast arrived, Hassan had surfed all of Francia's television news networks. The bombshell report from *Le Figaro* had led every broadcast.

Details of the story were the same on all the networks:

A conspiracy to secretly provide Virginia with *munitions biologique* had been traced to Francia's Prime Minister Jacques Demers. Also named in the report were Helen Levet, National Security Adviser to the PM, and General Regis LaFoy of the Armée de Francia. In a torrent of outrage at the accusations, Demers and Levet had issued vaguely worded denials. LaFoy's public statement, however, had undermined the responses of his alleged co-conspirators. "I believed my instructions regarding the munitions were legitimate orders," LaFoy had told *Le Figaro's* reporter.

As we scanned the channels over the course of the day, the story was picked up by news services across the globe. The reaction from the political class was swift.

The leader of the prime minister's opposition party in Francia called for a parliamentary investigation into "these reckless machinations." The consensus among heads of state the world over was best summed up by the prime minister of England who condemned the covert action as "dangerous and irresponsible." As expected, the premier of the USSR denounced the action in *Pravda*, calling it "another imperialistic abuse of a disadvantaged nation." Even Francia's hereditary president, Jérôme-Alexander Bonaparte, called the news "a blot on our national reputation if proven true."

"There's no harm in telling you now," Hassan said after they'd placed a call for dinner. "If we hadn't exposed the bloom conspiracy, my side was going to storm the armory in Charlottesville."

"And my side would have retaliated."

"Yeah," he said nodding his head. "The only winner of *that* war would have been the toads."

I felt a shiver of pride. Hassan and I had made a difference. We had averted a war. The bloom would almost certainly be removed from Virginia and the people responsible would be held accountable. Above all, we'd spared innocent lives. This was the kind of deed I'd dreamed about when I joined the Patrick Henrys. But surprisingly, this triumph had come with the help of an enemy.

When the room service waiter arrived, Hassan asked him to set up our table beside the television screen. Neither of us could get enough of the news reports.

Then, as we ate, the news team on a local Paris channel reported a murder. "Ludolph Eltz, a high-ranking member of Germany's Freedom Coalition party, has been shot dead in his apartment in the 17th Arrondissement. The police believe it was a burglary gone bad but have no suspects at this time," the perfectly coiffed anchor on the screen announced.

"Looks like the mechanic you hit on the head was unhappy with his employer," Hassan said.

I put down my fork and stared at the screen. In my elation over our sting, I'd forgotten about the German attack on the Arc de Triomphe – and the danger that still posed for Dot. "I need to leave for Caen – now," I said, rising from the table.

"I thought we agreed, Olivia. There's no need for you to rush out of Francia."

"That's not why I want to go there," I said, gathering my things.

"What's in Caen that's so important?"

"That's where the C-4 from Virginia is entering Francia."

"So?"

"I want to stop the attack on the Arc de Triomphe."

Hassan rose to his feet. "We're Britannics, Olivia. Why should we care if the Germans take down the Arc and start a war with the toads? That's not our fight."

"I'll do this alone if I have to, Hassan."

"Is this about Eltz?" he asked. "Was there something between you two?"

I scoffed. "God knows, he tried."

"So what's changed your mind about helping the Germans?"

I stared at the floor for a moment. "Dot destroyed the C-4 shipping documents with her name back in Virginia. But her name is still on the documents arriving in Caen."

"So what? Your comrade is already on the lam."

"I know that. But with Dot under suspicion, the toads will dig up anything with her name on it, anywhere in the world. That will lead them to the German's asset in Caen and their whole cover will fall apart. A fucking army of SS goons will hunt Dot down if she's connected to an attack on the Arc."

"You don't know that, Olivia."

"I've already put Dot in enough danger. She stuck her neck out for me and I'm not going to let it get worse," I said. "Look, I understand if you want to quit. You've done more than I ever expected."

Hassan rolled his eyes, then sighed. "Goddam it, woman. You are relentless," he said. "All right. We'll stop the Germans. But can I make a suggestion?"

"What?"

"We don't need to stop the entire attack on the Arc to keep Dot out of an SS investigation," he said. "All we need to do is destroy the shipping documents with her name on them."

"Isn't that the same thing?"

"Does a pickpocket work the same as a mugger?"

I nodded and smiled. "I see what you mean."

HIGHWAY 13, FRANCIA

The headlights of the blue sedan cast a wedge of light onto the highway that wound through the dark Normandy countryside.

Behind the wheel of the rental, Hassan glanced at the dashboard GPS. "Less than three hours until we reach the airport in Caen," he said. "We could have gotten your ID and passport if we'd waited until morning."

I shook my head. "The shipment arrives in the morning," I said. "We need to get there before the Germans pick up the C-4."

"Why did the Germans choose Caen? Paris has three airports. Any one of them would have been faster."

"The Freedom Coalition has an asset inside Customs at the Caen airport. He'll make sure the explosives pass through customs undetected."

As we drove under an overpass bridge, Hassan said, "You haven't told me much about the C-4. How was it shipped?"

"It's packed inside two bales of tobacco. The Germans set up a dummy import company to receive it."

"Clever," Hassan said. "Your idea?"

"Yeah," I said. "But the business address for the tobacco company is fake. I don't know where the Germans will unpack the C-4 from the bales – or how they're going to transport the explosives to the Arc. That's why we need to get there first and tail them."

"How do they plan to take down the Arc?"

"Eltz convinced me I didn't need to know the details," I said. "It made sense at the time – and he was right, the bastard. I could have blown their op if the toads arrested me and I talked."

"How much C-4 is coming in?"

"About five-hundred pounds in each bale."

Hassan's eyebrows rose. "Is that enough to bring down the Arc?"

"The Arc is supported by four pillars. If you take out one of them, the whole structure will collapse," I said. "Dot is an ordnance freak. She figured the whole thing out."

"I take it Dot is your friend in Virginia who supplied the C-4?"

"Shit," I said, my face tightening. This relationship with Hassan was dangerous. I'd let down my guard and put Dot at risk.

"Don't worry, Olivia. Dot's name is safe with me."

"You're asking me to put a lot of trust in you, Hassan. But it's all one sided."

After a long moment, he said, "My name is Brody."

"Brody?" I said, starting to laugh. "You're kidding me."

"Wish I was. My mother had a weakness for Australian soap operas."

"You don't look like a Brody," I said. "That means it must really be your name."

He laughed softly. "Yeah. Hassan sounds sexier, doesn't it?"

"You walk the walk pretty well in that department, Brody. Even with that goofy name."

***

I yawned, then looked at the dashboard clock. It was almost three AM. "I can take over the driving if you want to get some sleep, ... Brody." I still felt strange not calling him Hassan.

"Thanks, but without an ID, having you drive is too risky. If a gendarme stopped us... well, our options wouldn't be good ones."

"It's also risky having you fall asleep at the wheel."

"Then talk to me," he said.

"Where did you learn to speak French so well?"

"Hey," he said smiling. "When I said 'talk to me,' I wasn't asking for an interrogation."

"C'mon, Brody. Your dossier told you everything about me," I said. "It's *your* turn to spill."

Brody stared down the highway for a moment, then said, "I came to Francia as a kid with my mother. We lived here until she died when I was nine."

"I'm sorry to hear about your mother," I said. "Did you go back to your father in Pennsylvania?"

Brody shook his head.

"Then who took care of you back home?"

"I lived with foster families, mostly," he said.

"What happened to your father?"

Brody shrugged. "I don't know. Never met him."

"Oh," I said. "I'm sorry."

"Nothing to be sorry about," he said. "I was an accident of my mother's work. She took good care of me, though. She had high class clients and I never wanted for anything."

"Do you hate your father?"

"Not really," he said. "I've never thought much about him at all."

"It's strange," I said. "My dad was the perfect father. He took me and my brother with him everywhere when he was home on leave. We went hunting, fishing, to stock car races. But after he was killed in the war, I found myself hating him."

"How old were you when he died?"

"Eleven."

"Not a great age for dealing with grief."

I nodded, eyes welling. "I suppose you're right."

"But you still went into the military like he did."

"Yeah," I said. "Doesn't make much sense, does it?"

"You wanted to honor your father's sacrifice. That makes sense to me."

Dabbing my eyes, I said, "I've never told anyone... about hating my father after he died."

"I always lied about my mother's work," he said. "I guess that makes us even."

We both stared down the road in silence for a time.

Then I laughed softly. "Wow, what a cringey pair of spies we are."

"Yeah," Brody said with a pained smile. "My oversharing hangover is starting early."

Eager to change the subject, I studied the dashboard's GPS. "There's a highway service area coming up about a half-hour from Caen airport. I'd like to stop there."

"I thought you were in a hurry," Brody said. "We've still got plenty of fuel."

"I want to pick up some things at the truck stop ... a burner and maybe some better shoes," I said, nodding toward my feet. "These pink monstrosities are killing me."

2007

MUNCY, PENNSYLVANIA

Cora Duskin looked around her new quarters as the metal door clanged shut behind her. The four-by-eight-foot cell was illuminated by a single overhead bulb inside a metal cage. A bed frame bolted to the wall along with a steel sink and toilet were the only furnishings.

Cora ran her fingers over the bed's coarse wool blanket. Less than two months ago, she'd slept under an embroidered silk duvet at the Premier's Residence in Philadelphia.

She'd always known there were risks to a politician's life in the People's Republic of Pennsylvania. Still, the speed of her debacle had been stunning. The events that brought Cora from head of state to this cell began during a routine morning meeting with her chief of staff forty-seven days earlier.

Seated at the ornate Premier's Desk in the People's Palace, Cora downed a slug of coffee. "What's on my agenda today that I can skip, Lou?" she asked her chief of staff.

Standing before her, Lou Huber said, "Sorry. Nothing, ma'am."

"Don't bullshit me, Lou. I need to meet with a new donor from Erie. He's promising to bring—"

The phone on Cora's desk buzzed. She pressed the speaker button. "What is it?"

A female voice on the speaker said, "Sorry to interrupt, ma'am. I have General Williams on the line. He said it's urgent."

"Put him through," Cora said.

"Madam Premier," Pennsylvania's highest-ranking soldier said. "One of our artillery battalions near the border is shelling a fracking facility in Virginia without authorization."

"Who's responsible for this?" Cora asked, her face tightening.

"I don't know yet, ma'am. But I can assure you, the order to fire did not come from my headquarters."

Shit, Cora said under her breath, gripping the edge of her desk. This rogue attack could not have come at a worse time.

Last year, a huge shale deposit that spanned both sides of the border under Pennsylvania and Virginia had been uncovered through fracking. Eager for the lion's share of the oil and gas, each side had started drilling under the others' territory. Hoping a military bluff would stop the poaching, both countries had deployed troops to the area. The whole damned place was a powder keg.

"General, I want the shelling to stop immediately," Cora said into the phone. "Do you understand?"

"Ma'am, there's a possibility I may need to use force. Do I have your permission?"

Cora muted the phone and looked at her chief of staff. "What do you think?"

"Attacking our own troops could spark a mutiny," Lou said. "We don't know how deep this insubordination goes."

"Get my security council in here – now," she said to Lou, then unmuted the phone. "General, make every effort to stop the shelling. But do not attack our own troops unless you hear from me."

"Understood, ma'am," the general said, ending the call.

"I'll round up the members of the council," Lou said before leaving the room.

Cora exhaled slowly, then took a cigar from a wooden box on her desk and lit it with a chrome desk lighter. Nothing ever prepared you for this job – not even being raised in a shack in Romania with the threat of death as familiar as the smell of boiled cabbage. Her father's fear of the regime's ethnic cleansing brought him and his family here. Eager for immigrants from Europe, Pennsylvania was the only country that granted them visas.

Her reflection on the chrome lighter looked back at her. She was sixty-one but looked ten years older, her gray hair pulled back into a careless bun. Vanity was for politicians who begged the masses for votes. Cora was the 14th premier of Pennsylvania. Beginning with Morris Cooper, all of them had come to power without a public election.

In her world, looks did not matter. Taking care of your allies, winning the favor of those with money, being ruthless with your enemies, that's what got you into power – and kept you there

She was good at it, too. For eleven years she'd been premier, a job where only one of her predecessors had ever made it into double digits. In all that time, she'd managed to keep the peace with Virginia. But this dustup over the fracking facility was putting a lot at risk.

Exports from the new shale oil field were already bringing in hard currency. If that kept up, Pennsylvania and Virginia could join New York as the rich relations of the Britannic clan. But a war could wipe out all that wealth.

The phone on Cora's desk buzzed. She pressed the speaker button. "Yeah?"

"I've gathered the council, ma'am," Lou said.

"Bring them in," she said.

The five members of her National Security Council along with Cora's chief of staff shuffled into the office and found chairs around a long table.

"I trust Lou has briefed all of you on the situation," Cora said, taking a seat at the table's head. "Any suggestions?"

The minister of defense spoke first. "Ma'am, if an attack is already underway, let's take advantage of it. Our troops could get the drop on the virgies and push them back far enough to claim the entire shale field."

"Even if our troops succeed, Virginia will counterattack and drag us into a ruinous war," said the secretary of state. "There's too much at stake for the enemy to give up so easily."

"This is not the time to lose our nerve," the defense minister countered. "We can take—"

Cora cut him off. "I want to know why one of our artillery commanders disobeyed orders. What reason would he have for shelling the virgies and provoking a war?"

"Probably cracked under the pressure," said the secretary of state. "The troops have been on high alert for weeks."

The director of intelligence services leaned forward and tented his fingers. "We might want to look outside our borders for a motive."

"What do you mean?" Cora asked.

"Who stands to gain from a war between Pennsylvania and Virginia?" the spy chief asked.

Cora scowled. "Cut the crap, Henry. Tell us who you think is behind this."

"It could be Francia – or it could be the Soviets," Henry said. "Both countries would like to see us go to war. The fighting would weaken us and the virgies. The superpowers have bullied the Britannic states in the past. But the new wealth we stand to gain from gas and oil would make that harder for them."

"So what do you propose we do?" Cora asked.

"Apologize to the virgies, then publicly execute the rogue commander," Henry said.

"Anyone disagree?" Cora asked, her eyes sweeping the room for dissent.

The defense minister lowered his gaze, unwilling to challenge her.

"Lou, get me the president of Virginia on the phone," Cora said. "The rest of you are excused."

By the time her call reached Virginia's president, virgie troops had flooded over the border into Pennsylvania, crossing the Potomac in a carefully prepared offensive. Although the invasion quickly stalled, the damage to Cora's reputation was done.

Not long after Virginia's incursion began, Cora was detained by agents of the Justice Department. Cora had seen PRP leaders deposed before, they'd whimpered and begged. She went without a word.

The charges brought against Cora did not mention her decision at the border. Instead, she was accused of accepting bribes and fraud – charges that could have been brought against any officeholder in Pennsylvania. Her trial, held behind closed doors, was swift. The judge sentenced her to five years in prison.

The locked food slot in the door of Cora's cell opened. She turned and saw an envelope slip through the chute.

Cora opened the envelope, then burst into a bitter laugh after reading the note from her former chief of staff.

> *Take heart, Cora. The USSR has*
> *nominated you for the Nobel Peace Prize.*
>
> *Lou*

***

HARRISONVILLE, VIRGINIA

From a hastily dug foxhole beside the Harrisonville bridge, Major John Braxton squinted into the sunset. The two-lane road over the bridge, its pavement glowing in the last rays of light, disappeared into the shadows of a woodland a half mile away.

The orders for Braxton's company of the First Virginia Regiment were clear.

Defend the rural bridge over the Licking River. If forced to retreat, destroy the hundred-foot span.

Braxton's company was one of six deployed by the Army of Virginia across a 20-mile stretch of Pennsylvania – a corridor between the mountains that protected the bulk of Pennsylvania's fracking facilities. The Virginians had seized this prized territory after a lightning offensive across the Potomac that caught the pennies by surprise.

Now, with their supply lines stretched to their limits, the Virginians had to hold their prize. Reinforcements and supplies would not reach them for days.

Braxton looked around him. His men stared warily out of the foxholes dug near the bridge along the north bank of the river. Their eyes were fixed on the woods beyond the road. Everyone knew the pennies' counterattack would come from that direction.

Although Braxton had been a soldier since graduating from VMI, the last six days had been his first time under fire. His baptism into combat had been swift and brutal. He'd lost over a third of the 250 men assigned to his company – and three of his four officers.

He'd seen young men die, some quietly, others shrieking in agony. Stifling his compassion tore at him more than the thought of his own death. He'd made himself show a courage he didn't feel to keep the remaining troops from losing their nerve.

Braxton turned to the young lieutenant beside him. "Eugene, tell the demolition squad they've got ten minutes to finish wiring the bridge."

"Yes, sir," the lieutenant said before scrambling out of the foxhole.

With nightfall almost on them, Braxton walked along the entrenchments, scrounging for flares among his troops. Returning to his foxhole, he stashed the three flares he'd collected in an empty ammo box.

The sound of a vehicle approaching on the bridge behind him drew Braxton's gaze. A humvee stopped near the middle of the span and the commander of his battalion stepped out.

Braxton walked to the colonel and stood, waiting for his orders.

The colonel put a hand on Braxton's shoulder. "I have bad news, John. Your son was killed today. I'm very sorry."

Braxton closed his eyes and looked away. From the day Steve had enlisted, he'd tried to bury the thought his son would die. He needed to believe it was impossible. Now, Steve had become another of the boys he'd seen die, robbed of the years most people took for granted. Braxton felt a wail rise in his throat. He covered his mouth, holding it back. He could not command his troops without control of his feelings. Any signs of weakness would cost more lives.

Facing his commander again, he said, "How did it happen?"

"His unit was in Lewisburg. The foxhole he was in took a direct hit from a one-oh-five. Two other men died with him," the colonel said. "Look, John. I'm sending you to the rear. You need some time off the line."

"Sir, my company's been hit pretty hard. The only officer I have left is a twenty-year-old butter bar. He's not ready for this."

The colonel shook his head. "You're going back, John. That's an order."

"Then you better send for the MPs, sir. I'm not leaving."

The colonel exhaled slowly. "You've been out here too long. You need a break."

"If we don't hold this bridge, then my son died for nothing, sir. I need to stay."

"Are you sure?"

Braxton nodded. "I need to get back to my troops, sir. We still have some loose ends to tie down."

"Take care, John," the colonel said, extending his palm. "I'll be back tomorrow, hopefully with some replacements."

Braxton shook his hand. "I'll be here."

As the humvee pulled away, the lieutenant approached Braxton carrying a large spool of wire. "All the charges are primed, sir. Where do you want to set up the detonator?"

He pointed to an abandoned farmstead behind them on the road to the bridge. "Roll out the wire to that barn," Braxton said, then retrieved the detonator from his tunic and handed the device to the young officer. "Set it up to blow from there."

"Yes, sir," Eugene said and jogged away, wire unspooling behind him.

Braxton walked back to his foxhole. Fishing a lighter from his fatigues, he fired a cigarette and leaned back against the ground. The moment he'd been dreading had come. There was nothing to do but wait.

He'd lost a son today – and John could only blame himself. Following the Braxton tradition, Steve had joined the army the day he turned eighteen.

One year and two months. That's how long Steve lived after putting on a uniform. It didn't have to happen.

He could have discouraged Steve from being a soldier, pointed out the risks, the tedium, and the shitty pay. But he didn't. No, he'd been too full of pride in their precious family history. He'd dreamed of Steve being a part of that glory.

Instead of a hero, Steve was a dead nineteen-year-old who'd barely tasted life.

Losing his wife had been the deepest wound Braxton had known – until today. Ellen's death giving birth to Olivia now seemed like a fading dream, losing its significance as waking thoughts took hold.

Olivia... His baby girl was eleven now. After never knowing her mother, how would she take the death of her brother?

A wave of fear washed over John. What if Olivia decided to follow their family's military tradition as well? The way she'd grown up so far, it was certainly possible.

She'd been raised without a mother. She hunted, fished, and roughhoused. Hell, the girl loved dirt bikes and stock car races.

Braxton made a vow to himself in that moment. He would do everything possible to prevent Olivia from becoming a soldier. He'd sacrificed one child to the military. Steve would be the last.

Braxton stubbed out his cigarette.

But here and now, he had a job to do: protect the young soldiers under his command.

Braxton looked over the edge of his foxhole. Night had fallen, giving the pennies the advantage. The only thing his eyes could distinguish was land from sky.

The lieutenant dropped into their foxhole. "We're set to blow the bridge, major."

"Let's hope it doesn't come to that," Braxton said. "We need to send out two-man patrols to keep the pennies from getting too close, Eugene. Find a couple of—"

A chorus of shrill whistles rose in the distance.

"Incoming mortars! Take cover!" Braxton shouted to his troops.

The ground shook as the shells crashed around them in a thunderous volley. A few seconds later, another volley fell. Then one more.

When the shelling stopped, Braxton uncovered his

head, his ears ringing. Screams of pain and shouts for
a medic rose from the entrenchments around him.

Peering out of the foxhole, Braxton tapped the
lieutenant's shoulder and said, "Send up a flare."

A yellow streak rose into the darkness, then burst
into a glowing ball. Floating under a small parachute,
the flare bathed the ground with light.

Over a thousand armed men appeared in the field
beyond the bridge, their shadows weaving as they
advanced. The blinking of muzzle flashes from the
enemy ranks was followed by the thud of slugs striking
the ground around them.

Braxton swallowed hard. The pennies outnumbered
his depleted company four-to-one. A fight here would
be useless. They would be overrun and lose the bridge.
"Get the men ready to move back when the flare
dies," he said to the lieutenant.

Once the flare's light faded, Braxton began guiding
his men in an orderly retreat. His platoons laid down
covering fire in alternating bounds, allowing them to
fall back over the bridge without panic.

With only a few casualties, his company crossed
the bridge and took up defensive positions around the
farm on the other side.

They had only one objective left: destroy the
bridge.

Suddenly, the countryside lit up. The pennies had
launched their own flare.

Braxton saw the enemy was now on the far
riverbank, taking cover in the foxholes his men had
dug.

Under the light of the flare, the pennies could see
the bridge was unguarded. They would advance over
the bridge now, Braxton was sure of that.

When the flare burned out, Braxton said, "Get

ready to detonate the charges, Eugene."

"I'm ready, sir," the lieutenant said, holding the brick-sized device.

"Fire the charges," Braxton said calmly.

Braxton looked toward the bridge and instinctively winced, expecting the flash of the explosion.

Nothing happened.

"I don't know what's wrong, sir," the lieutenant said. "I've pressed the button three times."

"There must be a break in the wire," Braxton said. "We need to reconnect the detonator wherever it's broken."

"I'll find out where it is," the lieutenant said as he disconnected the detonator wire.

Braxton shook his head and took the detonator from the lieutenant. "No, you stay here, Eugene. Have all the men focus their fire on the bridge and pin the virgies down," he said, then grabbed the wire and began following it by feel in the dark.

Moving in a crouch, keeping his hand on the wire, Braxton trailed it toward the bridge. By their muzzle flashes, he could tell the pennies were almost halfway across the bridge but pinned down by the fire from his men.

"Where is the goddam break?" he muttered, scuttling like a crab. The clatter of the gunfire was a steady din, getting louder as he neared the enemy on the bridge.

On the sloping bank of the river, Braxton found the dead end of the wire. It was on the edge of a shell crater, severed by the blast. Braxton moved under the bridge, out of sight from the enemy, and fired his lighter. His men had rigged the wire below the deck of the bridge and there it was.

Dangling from the bridge's first pier was the live

end of the wire.

Carrying the detonator above his head, Braxton waded into the water. The river was chest deep when he reached the pier. Opening the jaws of the detonator, he inserted the wire and clamped it shut. The trigger light on the device glowed green.

He could hear footfalls above him. The enemy was moving across the bridge.

Braxton's finger paused over the red button.

The detonation would take less than a second. Once he pressed it, the bridge and all his regrets would be gone.

The night sky turned white as a roiling ball of flame rose over a hundred feet. As the glow of the fireball faded, John's troops cheered. They could see the bridge was gone.

John Braxton's unit succeeded in stopping the Pennsylvania counterattack that night. But Virginia did not win the war.

Outnumbered and cut off from their supply lines, the Virginians fell back to their own side of the Potomac.

Eventually dubbed the Second Pennsylvania-Virginia War, the conflict ended in a bloody stalemate. Before it was over, most of the fracking operations in both nations were destroyed.

~=~

| DAY NINE |

CAEN, FRANCIA

The windshield shook with the roar of an unseen jet as we neared Caen airport. Then a twin-engine plane rose above the hangars, a black shape against the orange dawn.

"That's the AirFrancia cargo terminal," I said, pointing toward a one-story warehouse across the main runway from Caen's passenger terminal.

The near corner of the cargo building was a lobby with a storefront sign. The rest of the terminal was fronted by ten numbered loading bays. The entire complex lay inside a high chain-link fence with a guarded gate.

I checked the time on my new burner from the truck stop. The display read: 5:50. Tucking the mobile back into my jacket, I was amazed at how incomplete I'd felt without a phone.

"Now that you've seen the layout, what's the plan?" Brody asked.

"We need to park where we can watch the loading bays. That's where the Germans will be picking up the bales."

"How will we recognize the Germans?"

"Their truck may be marked with their fake company. But in any case, I doubt anyone else will be loading exactly two bales of tobacco today."

"Hard to argue with that," Brody said.

I pointed toward an airline food service company opposite the cargo terminal. "Their employee parking lot looks like a good place to watch for the Germans."

"I'm on it," Brody said.

Once we were parked within sight of the loading bays, I said, "I doubt we'll have to wait long. They plan to deploy the C-4 at the Arc tomorrow."

"Tomorrow? That's a tight deadline. Any chance the Germans will delay the attack?"

"No way," I said. "Tomorrow is the date Frederick the Great became king of Prussia. The Germans want to remind the toads they were an independent nation once."

"If they're in a hurry, they might cut corners. That could help us."

"I hope you're right," I said, then looked down at my feet. "I'd hate to tail the Germans on foot, though. I'll be flip-flopping like a tourist at Chesapeake beach." I hadn't found any footwear better than shower slippers to replace my undersized pink trainers at the truck stop.

Brody smiled. "It's a good cover. Not many spooks work in their slippers."

"Why don't you get some sleep, wise guy? I'll take the first watch."

"All right. Wake me up in thirty minutes – if another plane doesn't beat you to it," he said, leaning back against the headrest and closing his eyes.

I watched the loading bays for the next two hours without rousing him. He slept through four takeoffs and landings.

***

Seated in the lobby of the AirFrancia cargo terminal, Mattias was getting nervous but trying not to show it. This clandestine assignment for the Freedom Coalition had him on edge.

He glanced at his coworker in the next chair. Arms folded across his chest, Oskar was in a stupor from the THC dab pen he'd been hitting in the step van all the way from Paris.

The two burly Germans in khaki workmen's jackets had been waiting in the lobby for nearly an hour. Neither of them understood the purpose of the bills of lading and customs forms they'd given the airline agent behind the counter. Their superiors at the Freedom Coalition had arranged all that.

Their instructions had been to retrieve two bales of tobacco arriving from Virginia with the rented step van they'd driven up from Paris. That seemed simple enough. But Mattias was certain there was some type of contraband inside the bales. Why else would they be posing as employees of a fake company?

Mattias cast a furtive look at the agent behind the counter. The man seemed absorbed with his computer. But that could be a ruse. Mattias was sure they looked suspicious. Well, Oskar did anyway.

His companion's shaved head was covered in crude tattoos and his ears pierced with hollow rings the size of a grape. He'd never met Oskar before they'd left Paris three hours ago. On the way, Oskar had casually revealed he had been recruited from a motorcycle gang.

Mattias leaned close to Oskar and whispered, "This is taking too long. I think they suspect something."

Oskar opened his eyes. "What makes you say that?" he muttered.

Afraid to share his thoughts about Oskar's looks, Mattias said, "Those cheap signs on our truck are a dead giveaway." Their white rental step van had magnetic signs on the doors that read: IMPORTATIONS DE TABAC BAUER.

"You worry too much, egghead. Grow some balls," Oskar said and closed his eyes again.

Mattias jumped in his seat when the phone behind the counter rang. The agent answered the phone, then looked at the Germans. Mattias was ready to bolt for the door.

The agent hung up the phone and motioned for them to approach the counter. "Thanks for waiting, gentlemen. Your shipment has cleared customs and all your paperwork is in order," he said. He then extended a clipboard over the counter and said, "If you'll please sign the release form, your cargo will be ready to load at bay number four."

Now confident they were not going to jail, Mattias stepped between Oskar and the agent. "I'll sign that," he said.

"Thank you, sir," the agent said after Mattias signed the form. "Here are your documents," he said, handing him a manila envelope.

Once the pair was outside, Oskar said, "Why did *you* sign the form? You were assigned to be the driver, not my superior."

"What difference does it make? I signed with the bogus name we were told to use."

"I'll take that," Oskar said, then grabbed the envelope with the documents and jammed it inside his jacket. "Our orders were clear. Neither of us is the leader," he insisted as they got into the truck.

"You were assuming authority."

Because you're a brain-dead oaf, Mattias wanted to say as he slid behind the wheel. Instead, he said, "Let's quit arguing and get this done."

After starting the step van, Mattias drove along the row of numbered truck bays.

A warehouse worker in an AirFrancia jump suit was waving to them from bay number four.

***

Shielding my eyes from the sun, I scanned the cargo terminal again. A white step van was backing up to bay number four. Squinting, I made out the company name on the door of the vehicle:

IMPORTATIONS DE TABAC BAUER

I recognized the dummy import company. "The Germans are here," I said, gently nudging Brody.

Opening his eyes, Brody saw a pair of beefy men in brown jackets step out of the van and climb the steps into the warehouse bay. "Looks like the Coalition sent their draft horses."

"That makes sense," I said. "The bales they're picking up weigh over seven-hundred pounds each – and that pair can muscle them out of the van with a hand cart. They won't need a warehouse with a forklift. They can unpack the explosives anywhere – even a residential garage."

Brody started the engine and backed the sedan out of its parking spot. "I'll get ready to tail them," he said driving toward the exit of the parking lot.

Ahead of them, the white step van turned onto the entrance ramp for the highway back to Paris. Following them about a quarter-mile behind, Brody said, "The best time to grab the documents will be before these guys deliver the explosives. Right now, we have only two to deal with. There's no telling how many Germans we'll find wherever they're taking the C-4."

"Can we somehow get these two to pull over along the highway?"

"That would draw the gendarmes. They always stop to assist a disabled truck. We'll need to wait until they're off the highway."

"They'll be in Paris in less than three hours," I said. "We better come up with a plan – and hope their van is low on gas."

"Or one of them has a small bladder," Brody added, smiling.

HIGHWAY 13, FRANCIA

The feud between Mattias and Oskar had been festering since the pair had left the cargo terminal in Caen an hour earlier.

After a halfhearted effort loading the bales, the biker had hit the flavored THC vape once they were on the road, filling the cab with a sickly cherry-scented cloud. Behind the wheel, Mattias was livid.

Neither man had spoken – until Oskar pointed to a highway exit sign and said, "Get off here. I need to piss."

"No," Mattias said, staring straight ahead. "Our orders were clear: Do not stop for any reason. That's why we were given food and drink for the trip."

"Who cares? We're making good time."

"It's not your place to decide that. Maybe it was normal to disobey orders in that motorcycle gang of yours. But you're working with the Coalition now. Hold your water – or use a bottle. I'm not stopping."

From his jacket, Oskar drew a retractable dagger. After

releasing the blade, he pressed it against Mattias's throat. "Listen, you pustule. Either you take the next exit, or I'll slice you from ear to ear and piss down your throat."

Turning the van onto the exit ramp, Mattias said, "We'll have to report this delay to Herr Wurten."

"Do that and you're dead. I guarantee it."

Mattias found a truck stop just off the highway and parked the van beside a convenience store near the petrol pumps. Oskar left the van and walked into the store. Alone in the vehicle, Mattias pounded on the steering wheel. "Who the hell does this idiot think he is?" he shouted.

Wiping his spittle from the wheel, Mattias was startled when a woman appeared outside the van and tapped on the window.

After Mattias rolled down the window, the blonde asked, "Do you know where to find a car's fuse box?" The woman then held out the owner's manual for her car. "It says here that a bad fuse could be the reason my car won't start."

Mattias was not comfortable talking to women. At the bookstore, he always let Harriet help the female customers. To make things worse, this woman was pretty. He stared at her, paralyzed.

"Would you mind taking a look at my car?" she asked, smiling.

Without speaking, he opened the door and followed the woman as she padded in house slippers toward a blue sedan parked in the row behind his van. In truth, Mattias knew little about cars. But he went anyway, mesmerized by her presence.

The woman opened the door to her car and pointed toward the dashboard. "The manual says the fuse box is somewhere under there. Can you help find it for me?"

Dumbstruck, Mattias got on his knees and peered under the

dash, then felt around with his hand.

"Would some light help?" she asked, handing him a torch.

Mattias took the flashlight and continued his search, contorting his large frame for a better view of the interior – with no idea what he was looking for amid the snarl of wires and connections under the dashboard.

After a couple of minutes, he felt the woman touch his leg. "I can see this is hopeless," she said as Mattias rose to his feet. "Thanks for your help. I'm sure you have better things to do."

Without a word, Mattias returned to their van. Then he saw Oskar walk out of the store.

Getting into the van, Oskar said, "Was that so bad? Now get us back on the road, egghead."

***

"No luck," Brody said after he slid into the driver's seat. "I looked for the documents all over that van – on the dashboard, the console, under the seats and the glovebox. Maybe with a little more time..."

"I saw the bald guy coming out of the men's room through the store window. I had to get you out of there." As our signal for Brody to bail on his search, I'd tossed a pebble against the back of the step van.

"I doubt these guys will stop again before they deliver the bales," Brody said, starting the car and resuming our tail on the Germans. "They had juice bottles and energy bars in the van."

"Yeah," I said. "Maybe it's time to switch from being pickpockets to muggers."

"That's not going to be easy."

"Surprising them somewhere isolated along the highway might work."

"We'd need to drive ahead of them and look for the right spot.

There's a good chance we'd blow our tail," Brody said. "And the driver has already seen you. So, no more damsel in distress games."

"I'm willing to risk that."

Brody drove in silence for a moment. "One other thing... These guys may be armed. Are you ready for wet work?" he asked. "Because it may come to that."

I mulled his question. Could I bring myself to kill someone in cold blood? In all my years in uniform, I'd never fired a shot outside a training exercise. Now, I might need to look someone in the eyes and take their life. "I watched you do it at the night club," I finally said. "Is it hard?"

"I hate it," Brody said.

"Yet you killed those SS agents without hesitating."

"Before I started down that alley, I reminded myself of the number of people who might die if they captured you."

"Maybe I should do the same,"

"Whatever you do, be sure you're ready. Because if you take this on and hesitate, you'll be throwing away both our lives."

I paused for a moment. "I'd do it to protect Dot," I said, "and I'd do it to protect you."

Brody looked into my eyes. "Then I'm ready, too."

***

Behind the wheel of the van, Mattias reached across the console and tapped Oskar on the shoulder. "That's them again," he said as the blue sedan passed them in the left lane.

"Are you back on that?" Oskar said, opening his eyes.

"It's the same car, I tell you – and the same woman. She asked me to fix her car back at the truck stop," Mattias said. "And now she's got a *schwarze* driving the car."

"So what?"

"Why do they keep speeding up and then slowing down?"

Oskar shrugged. "*Schwarzes* are terrible drivers. Everybody knows that."

"I'm worried they may be police. I don't know what we're really hauling for the Coalition, but I'm sure it's not legal."

"You read too many fucking books."

"I think we should call Herr Wurten before we get to Paris. We could be bringing the police with us."

Oskar reached into his jacket, drew his dagger and released the blade. "You'll keep your mouth shut. You understand?" he said, polishing the serrated blade on his sleeve. "Nobody is telling Wurten we stopped along the way."

PARIS, FRANCIA

After tailing the step van for nearly three hours, Brody and I hadn't found a place to overpower the Germans without attracting the police. Twice, Brody had passed the van and waited along a deserted stretch of highway only to find vehicles coming in the opposite direction when the Germans caught up to us.

Now, as the day neared noon, the Germans had taken an exit from the highway into an industrial district on the outskirts of Paris. After a half-mile on the two-lane road, the van entered the gate of a self-storage facility.

"This could be their staging area for the attack," I said.

Brody drove past the gate to avoid tipping off their surveillance and stopped at an abandoned petrol station across the road. "Not an easy nut to crack," he said, studying the site.

Surrounded by a steel spike fence, the compound had two

identical buildings, each with a dozen storage units. Every unit had a green pedestrian door with a large numeral and a double-wide vehicle door beside it. There wasn't a window in sight.

"Looks like they're in unit five," I said as the van stopped and sounded the horn outside the garage door.

"Watch carefully when they open the door," Brody said. "This might be our only chance to see what they're up to."

The first thing I noticed when the garage door rose was a silver SUV parked inside the storage unit. In a back corner, I caught a glimpse of a camp table laden with an assortment of items, fronted by a folding chair. A man appeared in the garage. He gave the step van driver hand signals, guiding it alongside the SUV. Then the garage door closed.

"If we decide to storm the place, the odds are two on three," I said, then looked at the time on my phone. "We have about eleven hours to make our move. The Germans won't launch the attack until midnight at the earliest. Tomorrow's date is important to them."

"The first thing they'll need to do is remove the C-4 from the tobacco bales. That'll keep them busy for a while," Brody said.

"Eltz didn't share any details on this op, but I gathered they want to get a vehicle with the C-4 close to one of the pillars before detonating," I said. "I don't see the Germans blowing someone up along with the vehicle, though. A suicide attack is not their style. So one of the lugs from the step van is going to pull a park-and-dash at the Arc."

"My guess is they're going to load the explosives on the SUV," Brody said. "The step van has already been seen at the airport in Caen and can be traced back to them."

I nodded. "That makes sense."

Brody pointed toward the sign at the entrance to the storage facility. Along with the name *Entreposage Barbier* the sign included a phone number. "I'll call the management and schedule a tour," he said. "We should get a look inside one of those units."

"Before we do that, I'd like to get something to eat — and replace these fucking slippers," I said, nodding toward my feet.

Brody smiled. "Too bad. I was starting to like the look."

***

Seated before his laptop on a folding chair, Karl Wurten tested the signal between his smartphone and the detonator for the third time. When his computer confirmed the connection, Wurten struck a flame with his lighter, relit a meerschaum pipe and smiled. An engineer could never become complacent — especially a German one.

The makeshift workstation Wurten had created in the storage unit on a portable table was unassuming. But it was the nerve center of an operation that could change the history of Europe.

As Wurten prepared for another system test, a claxon sounded outside. He walked to the front of the storage space and pressed the button to open the garage door. The brutes were back.

Other than their bulk, Wurten questioned the wisdom of his superiors at the Coalition in selecting these two. Mattias was soft-headed and Oskar a common thug. The Coalition was led by men of ideas, he reminded himself. Finding the muscle for this mission had not been easy.

"You are over twenty minutes late. Why?" Wurten said to Mattias and Oskar after they'd parked the step van.

The men looked at each other. Then, Oskar said, "They took a long time with the paperwork at the cargo terminal."

"Where are the documents?" Wurten asked.

Oskar reached into his jacket and handed Wurten the envelope. "This is everything they gave us."

Wurten opened the envelope and examined the bills of lading and customs forms. "Everything looks in order. Follow me," he said, then led the men to his workstation.

Opening the briefcase on the folding table, Wurten placed the documents inside. He would need to be reimbursed by the Coalition for the shipping costs. He then unzipped a nylon satchel on the table.

"We have reached a critical stage of our mission," Wurten said as he took three Walther pistols from the satchel. "As a precaution, we will be armed at all times from this point forward," he said, handing each man a weapon. To have armed this inept pair any sooner would have been inviting trouble.

"This is a fine piece," Oskar said, examining the weapon before tucking it into his jacket.

"Made in Germany, of course," Wurten said, then gestured with his pipe toward the step van. "Now, get the bales out of the vehicle."

As the pair began unloading the step van, Wurten refilled his pipe and struck a flame. That Ludolph Eltz had been killed during a robbery had come as no surprise, he thought, puffing on his pipe. Eltz was a pretentious fool who had risen in the Coalition through his inherited fortune.

Still, Wurten grudgingly admitted Eltz had helped the Coalition by finding some useful idiots among the nics to provide the explosives. But he would need to inspect the C-4 carefully once it was removed from the bales. Nics were notoriously incompetent.

"The bales are unloaded, Herr Wurten," Mattias called out.

Wurten approached the men. "Cut the bindings and strip away

the burlap," he said. Then, Wurten directed the men in carefully dissecting the bales. Over an hour later, they had two plastic-wrapped bundles and a large, pungent pile of tobacco.

Wurten sliced through the plastic wrapping on one of the bundles and smiled. Each of the individually wrapped blocks was labeled: *Explosifs - Armée de Francia*. The nics had come through. Although he was disappointed it wasn't bloom, this was high-quality ordnance.

Mattias' eyes widened. "Is that dynamite?" he said, fear in his voice.

"Something like that," Wurten said. "But you needn't be afraid," he said, then picked up one of the blocks and tossed it on the floor in front of Mattias.

The big man cringed in terror.

Wurten laughed. "It will only detonate with a blasting cap. Even a bullet will not set it off."

"What a pantywaist," Oskar said, joining in the laughter.

"Enough joking," Wurten said. "Move the explosives into the back of the SUV. I'll show you how to pack them."

Mattias was still shaken. "If we're making a car bomb, who is going to drive it?"

Wurten smiled. "No one," he said, then pulled the smartphone from his pocket and typed a command. The headlights on the SUV turned on and the engine started. "When the time comes, this vehicle will deliver our little surprise to the Arc de Triomphe all on its own and then detonate." As a backup to his laptop, Wurten had enabled the mission to launch from his mobile.

Mattias gasped as Wurten turned off the engine. "My God, Herr Wurten. This will strike a glorious blow for our fatherland."

***

The rental agent pointed to the pin pads by the door into storage unit 11. "This pad opens the pedestrian door and this one opens the garage door," he said, then tapped in the entry code.

After stepping inside, the agent flipped the light switch. "Our units are climate controlled and have full electrical connections. The garage door is motorized and large enough for two vehicles," he said, leading us inside the empty space.

Brody and I made a peculiar pair.

Wearing a backpack over a black jumpsuit with rubber-soled combat boots, I looked like a ninja. Meanwhile, Brody favored a tourist at the Louvre, with chinos, polo shirt and tennis shoes. I'd insisted we go shopping before the rental unit appointment.

"I was surprised to hear you rent these units by the day," I said, studying the construction. The walls and roof were ribbed sheet metal, the floors a concrete slab. Cheap, but impenetrable.

"We sometimes get couples and small groups interested in using our units for a party space," the agent said with a smirk. "Whatever you do here is your business. But I should add that we'll be forced to charge for any cleaning that's necessary."

Brody strayed back to the door, checking out the lock. The simple deadbolt style was one he could pick in seconds.

The rental agent pointed toward the ceiling. "As you can see, our units have exposed supports. Some of our day renters find them handy for attaching ...ahem, appliances."

"What kind of appliances?" Brody asked.

Leering, the agent said, "I'll leave that to your imagination."

"We'll take it," I said.

Brody seemed surprised by my decision, but he pulled out his wallet. "Will you take a credit card?" he asked the agent. After charging Brody's card on his smartphone, the agent left.

"I thought we were just scouting," Brody said.

"The Germans are six units away. Why not crash their party from here?" I said, then reached into my backpack and took out a makeup compact. "I'll rig a mirror by the door so we can watch their unit."

Brody nodded. "Smart move."

Walking toward the front of the unit, I said, "I'll open the garage door so you can bring the car inside."

***

Wurten turned the camera hidden in the SUV's luggage rack a few degrees, then walked back to his laptop to inspect the adjustment. The self-driving vehicle now had a clear line of sight on both sides of the road.

He was proud of his work disguising the auto-drive sensors. To the untrained eye, the SUV looked like any other vehicle on the road. But camouflaging its autonomous capability was not enough to avoid the most serious problem the vehicle would encounter: the irrationality of human drivers. Their flouting of traffic laws often confounded driverless vehicles into a standstill.

That's why he'd chosen 4 AM as the time to launch the attack. There would be less traffic on the roads. As a bonus, security would be light at the Arc as well.

Another of Wurten's triumphs was the logistics of the detonation. After studying satellite images online, he'd discovered a weakness in the monument's security. The Arc was not perfectly placed inside its circle of anti-vehicle barriers. The knee-high concrete columns were less than six meters away from the structure at its northwest corner, close enough for the explosion of the SUV to destroy that pillar and bring down the Arc. In fact, Wurten had programmed the exact coordinates of that spot on the vehicle's GPS as the signal to detonate the C-4.

The bomb itself was another masterwork. Knowing there was a chance the driverless vehicle might be captured, Wurten had boobytrapped the device by using redundant wiring in the detonation system. Cutting the wrong wire would trigger the explosion. Even turning off the vehicle or disabling its auto-drive would ignite the bomb.

While Mattias and Oskar swept the last of the tobacco onto a tarp, Wurten closed the laptop and summoned an eCAB on his phone. With six hours until their 4AM launch, everything was ready. There was time for a good meal and some sleep. His head had not touched a pillow in more than twenty-four hours.

Wurten walked to where the two men were sweeping. "I'm leaving for a few hours," he said. "Mattias, you're going with me. Oskar, you stay here."

Oskar looked dejected. "Why do I have to stay?"

"You're the best guard we have," Wurten answered.

"Why does *he* get to go?" Oskar grumbled, nodding toward Mattias.

"Because I need a guard as well," Wurten said, then looked at his phone. "Come, Mattias. The eCAB is almost here."

***

"An eCAB just pulled up," I called out from my post by the door of the storage unit. "Two of the Germans are leaving."

Lounging on the hood of the sedan with his back against the windshield, Brody jumped to his feet. "This could be the time to make our move. The odds are on our side."

"I agree."

Heading for the door, Brody pulled the pistol from his jacket and raked a round into the chamber. I did the same before we stepped outside.

We'd already discussed our assault. Once we reached the Germans' storage unit, Brody would quietly pick the lock on the pedestrian door and then lead the way inside. I would cover him from the doorway.

The element of surprise and superior numbers were in our favor.

We both believed they would be enough.

***

Mattias was torn as he squeezed his big frame into the eCAB. Without Oskar around, should he tell Herr Wurten about the car that seemed to follow them from Caen?

"Move over, *dummkopf*," Wurten said as he slid into the back seat of the compact sedan beside Mattias.

Staring out the window as the eCAB left the storage facility, Mattias was haunted by guilt. He was a believer in Germany's destiny of greatness. That's why he'd joined the Freedom Coalition. Being a part of Herr Wurten's mission had filled him with pride. But that mission might be undone by his own cowardice. As they neared their hotel, he could not hold back any longer.

His eyes on the floor, Mattias leaned toward Wurten and spoke in a whisper. "I think we may have been followed on our drive back from Caen."

"What?" Wurten said, eyes flashing angrily. "Who was following you?"

Still whispering, Mattias said, "A woman and a *schwarze* in a blue sedan. The woman asked me to fix her car at a truck stop. I saw the same car pass us twice on the highway from Caen."

"Why didn't you tell me this before?"

"Oskar pulled a knife and made me stop so he could piss," Mattias whined softly. "Then he threatened to kill me if I told you."

Wurten scowled in disgust. "You are *both* worthless," he said, then leaned forward and grabbed the driver's shoulder. "Take us back – now!"

***

I stood beside Brody as he picked the door lock of the Germans' storage unit. The ominous heft of the pistol in my hand brought back the vow I'd made on taking a life. *I'd do it to protect Dot... and to protect you*, I'd assured Brody. The next few minutes might test my resolve.

"The door's unlocked," Brody whispered. "Get ready."

My heart pounding, I brought the weapon to eye level, ready to fire, as Brody crouched and slowly opened the door.

My mouth fell open as I peered inside. Near the back of the space, beside the step van and the SUV, one of the burly Germans was asleep on a folding chair, his feet on a table.

Brody and I glanced at each other, astonished by our luck.

Our weapons trained on the German, we walked softly toward him. About ten paces away, Brody called out. "Hands up!"

Startled, the German fell out of his chair. "Don't shoot! Don't shoot!" he said from the floor, holding out his palms.

"Face down on the floor! Spread your arms!" Brody ordered. "If he moves, put a hole in him," he said to me. Brody then frisked the German and took his pistol.

With the big man under control, I tucked my gun away. "Where are the shipping documents for the bales you picked up?" I asked him.

"I don't know what you're talking about."

I turned toward Brody and winked. "He doesn't know. Go ahead and shoot him."

"Wait!" the German said. "The documents are in the briefcase on the table."

After opening the briefcase, I smiled. On top of a sheaf of papers was an envelope with an Air Francia logo. Inside were the shipping documents. Putting the envelope into my pocket, I said, "I've found the papers. Let's get out of—"

***

"Drop your weapon!" Wurten shouted at the *schwarze*, stepping inside the door.

Sensing a chance to escape, Oskar rose from the floor and ran toward Wurten and Mattias.

"Get out of the way, fool!" Wurten shouted at Oskar who was now blocking his shot at the intruders. Seizing the opportunity, the man and woman took cover behind the step van.

As Oskar reached the other Germans, the *schwarze* fired three shots toward them. Unharmed but terrified, the three Germans retreated outside the doorway.

"That was the woman and the *schwarze* from the truck stop," Mattias said.

"We need to go in there and finish them," Wurten said. "We cannot let these vermin derail our mission."

"They took my gun," Oskar said, raising his palms.

"Here," Wurten said, snatching the pistol from Mattias and handing it to Oskar. "This oaf is too stupid to use it."

"Let's call for help," Oskar said. "We've got them cornered."

"There is no time," Wurten said. "The gunfire will bring the police."

"I have an idea," Mattias said hesitantly.

Wurten turned toward him, his face twisted with disgust. "What?"

"We can still save the mission, Herr Wurten," Mattias said, then pointed to the pin pad for the garage door on the outer wall. "Open the door and launch the vehicle now."

***

Huddled behind the step van, Brody and I peered toward the doors at the front of the storage space. There were only two ways out: the pedestrian door and the garage door.

"We can't stay here much longer," I said. "Your shots are going to bring the police."

"I know. But I had to fire to make them retreat."

"They'll probably make a move on us soon," I said. "The Germans don't want to be here when the police arrive any more than we do."

Brody looked through the back window of the SUV parked beside them. A large bundle of explosives filled the floor of the rear compartment. "They've already got the primer and a remote signal device on that load. This package is ready to blow."

"I don't like being a sitting target. I think it's time for a breakout," I said, slipping into military jargon.

"Agreed. Bounding overwatch?"

I raised my gun. "Yeah, I'll move to the garage door. You cover my move, then join me," I said. "We'll set up a base of fire and then open the door."

As I started a dash toward the entrance, the garage door rumbled and began to open. "Dammit," I said, ducking behind the SUV. "Looks like we're playing defense."

Using the sport vehicle for cover, we both took firing positions and waited.

Olivia was startled when the SUV's engine growled into life. "What the hell?"

Brody peered inside the driver's compartment. An array of sensors on the controls were blinking in succession. "Shit. That looks like a system check. This thing is rigged to drive itself."

I was startled for a moment. Then I saw an opportunity. I opened the driver's door and slipped inside. Crouching below the windows, I called out to Brody. "Get in."

"Are you serious? What if they see us inside?"

"So what? They're not going to shoot their assault vehicle."

"Why not? The C-4 won't detonate from gunfire."

"Yeah, but an SUV full of bullet holes is going to draw the attention of the police."

"You are totally berserk," Brody said, then got in and hunkered down beside me.

"Stay down and keep your gun trained on the doors," I said as the SUV began to move.

To my relief, the vehicle rolled out of the storage space, unhindered.

Once we'd left the rental complex, Brody exhaled slowly and put away his gun. "Now, all we need to do is get off this time bomb before it explodes."

***

Taking cover behind the corner of the garage door, Wurten felt a moment of regret as he watched the SUV leave the storage unit. The Arc de Triomphe would not topple on the anniversary of Frederick the Great's coronation. But it would be destroyed, all the same. Their liberation movement would still achieve a glorious victory.

Now, to ensure the security of their mission, they needed to eliminate the intruders still inside the storage unit. Fortunately, he had a plan.

"They're hiding behind the step van. Aim for the petrol tank and keep firing," Wurten said to Oskar. "The tank is just behind the driver's door." Raising his own pistol, Wurten began to fire.

As the bullets pierced the van's body, fuel began to spill on the floor.

"Nothing is happening," Oskar said after three shots.

"Keep firing," Wurten ordered, then fired two more rounds.

With a large pool of petrol now on the floor, Wurten pulled out his lighter, locked on the flame, and tossed the lighter toward the van. With a loud *whoomp*, the interior of the storage space was engulfed in flames.

"Come," he said, leading his underlings away. "They'll never get out alive."

***

When the SUV stopped for a red light at a deserted intersection, Brody opened the driver's door and stepped out of the vehicle. "C'mon, Olivia," he said, waving to me. "This is our stop."

Instead of getting out, I climbed over the console and into the rear compartment. "I think there's enough time to disarm this thing," I said, examining the explosive device.

The bomb filled most of the space below the rear windows of the SUV. Centered atop the neatly bundled blocks of C4, a battery powered detonator spread a spiderweb of wires to an array of blasting caps.

"No-no-no-no, Olivia," Brody said from the street. "You can't be serious."

"Go," I said, waving him away. "I can do this alone."

"Why in the hell are you trying to stop the attack?"

"I don't have time to explain," I said, crouching over the detonator. "Go, before the light turns green."

Brody sighed, got back into the vehicle and closed the door. "I'm not leaving. So please tell me why you're doing this?"

My eyes on the detonator, I said, "The German attack is going to bring back an old blood feud with Francia. Thousands will die and nothing will change – just like the wars between Virginia and Pennsylvania." I turned toward Brody, looking into his eyes. "Where things have gone between us... That's helped me see that," I said. "I never thought this could happen between enemies."

Brody touched my face. "Then you've got my help – for as long as you want it."

I smiled. Then turned toward the detonator again. "Keep your eyes open for the police. If we get stopped, they'll arrest us before I can disarm the explosives."

As the vehicle began to roll again, Brody looked at the bomb and said, "I've never seen a timer like that before."

"It's not a timer," I said, pointing to the seven digits on the electronic gauge. "The detonation is set for a GPS coordinate. I've been watching. The numbers only change when we move. This thing will explode at a place, not a time."

"No problem, then. I'll kill the engine," Brody said, reaching for the dashboard.

"Wait!" I said, grabbing his arm. "Anyone clever enough to build this thing wouldn't let it be disabled that easily. Look," I said, pointing to a wire along the floor from the detonator to the dashboard. "Turning off the vehicle will probably trigger the bomb."

Brody nodded toward the detonator. "If that's a GPS device, I'm certain that it's set to explode at the Arc de Triomphe. What if we drive somewhere else?"

"I think disabling the auto-drive controls will trigger it, too."

"Shit," Brody said, looking out the window. "We'll be at the Arc in less than ten minutes with traffic this light."

"I can figure this thing out before we get there."

From my training as an ordnance officer, I knew the workings of an explosive device were always the same: a detonator would send an electrical charge to a set of blasting caps that would ignite the explosive charges. Of course, every bombmaker understood those principles were well known. So they tried to disguise the connections of their devices. Sometimes, they also boobytrapped them. I would need to be careful.

"Give me the key to your rental car," I said, holding out my hand.

Brody pulled the key from his pocket. "What are you going to do?" he asked, handing it to me.

"I need something that will cut electrical wire. The teeth of the key will do that."

"Do you know which wires to cut?"

"Not yet," I said, studying the maze of wires around the detonator. This bombmaker was devious. There were two and sometimes three wires connecting all the elements. Cutting the wrong wire would trigger the bomb.

A car horn blared behind us, breaking my concentration. I looked up. "What's happening?"

"We're stuck," Brody said, pointing through the windshield. In the roundabout ahead of us, a plastic bag fluttering in the wind had snagged on the reflector in a lane marker. "This damned auto-drive doesn't know what to make of that bag and it won't budge."

The car behind them blasted the horn again.

"We can't stay here any longer," Brody said, getting out of the vehicle.

I watched as Brody untangled the bag, then walked back toward the SUV with his palm out like a matador approaching a bull. He knew the vehicle would not move if it detected a human.

"You slayed that," I said as Brody got back into the driver's seat.

"Any progress?" he asked as the SUV entered the roundabout.

"I'm getting closer," I said, turning back to the detonator.

"Oh, shit," Brody said as the red and blue lights of a police car began flashing behind them. "That asshole stuck behind us must have called the gendarmes."

"I need more time, Brody."

"We're coming to a red light," he said as the SUV slowed down. "After I get out, move into the driver's seat. I'll go back to the cops and draw them away."

"Roger that," I said, climbing out of the cargo area.

When the SUV stopped, Brody stepped out of the vehicle and said, "I'll meet you at the Arc."

From the driver's seat, I watched as Brody walked toward the police car behind me.

***

Brody flashed The Smile as he approached the cruiser. "I'm real sorry we stopped up the traffic, officer," he said to the cop behind the wheel in a thick Britannic accent. "Me and my girl, we had a fight. She is really mad with me."

"Not my problem," the policeman said in a frosty voice.

Brody looked behind him. "Oh. She's drivin' away," he said feebly. "Come back, honey! Come back!" he called out.

The policeman shook his head in disgust and killed his emergency lights.

"Can y'all take me home?" Brody asked. "I live over in Montmarty."

"Call an eCAB," the gendarme said, then turned the cruiser around and sped away.

Alone on the street, Brody watched the SUV recede in the distance. Olivia was unbearably stubborn. And that, goddammit, was why he'd fallen in love with her.

Reaching for his phone, he hailed an eCAB to the Arc de Triomphe.

***

As the SUV moved away, I looked behind me. The red and blue lights of the cruiser stopped flashing. Then I lost sight of Brody in the glare of the streetlights. Would I ever see him again? I pushed the thought aside and crawled back into the rear of the SUV with the bomb.

The time had come for a decision. I had finally isolated the two wires that connected the detonator to the battery. Cut the right one and I would defuse the bomb. Cut the wrong one and I would ignite a half-ton of explosives. I had no clue which choice was right.

I grabbed the car key to cut the wire, then scanned the street ahead of me. If I had no control over my fate, at least I could find a place where a mistake would cause the least harm.

The SUV was making its way through a brightly lit street lined with apartments when I spotted a dark area ahead. A park maybe? This might be the place to make my move.

As the vehicle got closer to the darkened area, I chose one of the wires and placed the teeth of the keys against it. Looking outside, I saw the dark outlines of tombs. A cemetery. Just perfect.

I took a deep breath, then cut the wire.

| DAY TEN |

The television in room 302 at the Hotel Durant was tuned to the BBC news. Sprawled on the bed, facing the ceiling, Brody ignored the broadcast. His thoughts were on Olivia.

In a matter of days, she had changed him.

Over time, the adrenaline rush of his work had numbed him. Feeling nothing had become normal. Finding Olivia had revealed the emptiness in his life. For that alone, he was grateful to her.

But Olivia had given him more than that. She'd shown him another measure of courage... the courage to admit she'd been wrong, and the courage to right it.

He'd been lucky to find her, even if she'd been an enemy – especially since she'd been an enemy. Their time together had brought another realization: No matter what flag we saluted, we were more alike than different.

Now, he was ready for a change in his life. He'd done more than his share of wet work, had grown weary of surviving on lies. From this day on—

"Hey!" Olivia called out from the bathroom. "Did you forget about me?"

Walking into the tiled room, Brody found her wearing two towels, one wrapped around her head, the other her torso. The tops of her breasts and her slim legs were wet and gleaming. The sight cleared his fog of introspection. "I'm a fan of the view," he said with a grin.

"Simmer down, tomcat. Last night wasn't enough?"

"Never. But I'll take a rain check." Their lovemaking after returning from the Arc de Triomphe had left them both exuberantly spent.

As Olivia removed the towel from her head, Brody donned a pair of plastic gloves and uncapped a plastic bottle of hair dye. With both of them facing the mirror above the sink, he began working the dye into her hair. "You're going to look good as a brunette in your new passport photo."

"Not sure I care for my new name, though."

"Oh? What's wrong with Agnes Butcher?"

"Do you really have to ask?"

"Listen," he said, stopping his work. "I think the BBC has another report."

In the usual RP accent, the voice of the television announcer carried into the bathroom. "Law enforcement officials in Paris report that no one has yet claimed responsibility for the unexploded bomb found in a vehicle parked near the Arc de Triomphe. In other news from Paris, newly elected prime minister Charles Pascal has formed a new government after the ouster of his predecessor following the so-called Bloom Scandal. Pascal has promised to begin bilateral peace talks with the premier of Pennsylvania and the president of Virginia."

"The Germans still haven't taken credit," Brody said, applying the dye again.

"I'm not surprised. Failure is always a bastard."

Brody continued the dyeing in silence for a time, then said, ""Any idea what you'll do after you get to England?"

"I never thought I'd get this far."

Brody stopped applying the dye. "I'm done," he said.

"I think you missed some spots above my ears."

"No, I mean I can't go back to work for the PRP."

Olivia turned to face him. "Why not? What you did to help me will never get back to your boss."

"I know that."

"Then why quit? You said it yourself, you love feeling alive."

"That isn't true anymore."

"What we did made *me* feel alive."

"Yeah. But what difference did it make?"

"We saved innocent lives. Maybe thousands of them."

"That won't stop our countries from slaughtering more. All the misery caused by politicians boils down to one thing... convincing someone that it's patriotic to do something terrible. I don't want to be that guy anymore. What you did helped me see that."

"I was only trying to save myself – and Dot."

"In the end, you had the courage to admit you were wrong in helping the Germans," he said. "Olivia, I've got six days before my boss expects me back. If I quit now, they'll never find me. There's only one thing holding me back. Will you come with me?"

Olivia slowly wrapped her arms around his waist. "Try and stop me," she said.

2076

NEW YORK, NEW YORK

On a raised scaffolding at the back of Hamilton
Square Garden, the Chinese reporter stood before a
robot camera and adjusted his lapel mic. "It's getting
loud in here. How is the ambient sound?" he asked his
producer in Mandarin.

From a Beijing studio, the producer replied through
the reporter's earpiece. "Your audio is good, Wuhao.
We're filtering out most of the crowd noise," she said.
"Move a step to your right. We want to get more of
the floor in the shot when we go live."

The reporter complied, revealing a bird's eye view
of the convention.

Surrounding a central podium, seven tables
were arranged in a semi-circle. At each table, six
representatives from every Britannic country sat
around a small national flag. Near the tables were
platoons of aides in folding chairs. The public filled

the stadium seats behind the aides.

The gathering was in recess and the din of nearly 10,000 voices echoed through the fifth incarnation of Hamilton Square Garden. International coverage of the event was being broadcast in 24 languages by China's CCTV, the only remaining worldwide news organization.

"We're going live at the top of the hour. Are you ready?"

Wuhao nodded. "Shì de."

"Very well," the producer said. "We're live in 5-4-3-2-1…"

A chyron banner on the screen below the reporter read: THE BRITANNIC DECISION. "Welcome to CCTV's live coverage of this historic event from New York," Wuhao said in English. "Tonight, after weeks of negotiations, delegates of the Britannic nations of North America will vote on ratification of the American Union, an agreement that, if approved, will create a measure of unity among these seven nations for the first time."

Wuhao gestured to the empty podium behind him. "We expect a vote once the speaker of the congress appears at the podium. In the meantime, we're going to speak to Dorothy Braxton-Linn, professor of Britannic history at Columbia University."

On a split screen, an attractive forty-something woman in her living room appeared beside the reporter. Wuhao said, "Professor, for most of their history, these seven nations have been at odds with each other. What finally brought them together?"

Dorothy smiled. "I would say necessity more than anything."

"Was there a turning point in this change in their relationships?"

"I think the bilateral talks of Virginia and Pennsylvania with Francia's prime minister Pascal was the first time relations in the region moved past a cease fire mentality. The Treaty of Paris that followed those talks allowed observers from each nation to monitor foreign military build-ups near their borders. That relaxed the defense posture of all the nations in the region. That was fine with the Franks. They had their hands full putting down the uprising in Germany."

"Some pundits have said the collapse of the Soviet Union in 2049 was a factor."

"Certainly," she said. "Pennsylvania lost a huge source of subsidies and preferential trade deals. Other nations in the region also felt the economic pain. But the allies of Francia in the region also suffered. Without an existential foreign threat, Francia became hyper-partisan and isolationist. They lost interest in the region. More importantly, Francia's subsidies and investments in the Britannic region declined."

Wuhao's eyes widened. "That's surprising. Can you explain how an economic decline led to better relations between these nations?"

"Many of the region's leaders had become wealthy and powerful by serving the interests of Francia and the Soviets. When the foreign money dried up, so did the base of power for these leaders. Not long after that, reform movements sprang up in Virginia, Pennsylvania and New York. Their smaller neighbors also caught the reform fever. That led to the first meeting of the Reform Council in 2051 when dissidents from all seven nations met in New York."

"What were the goals of these reformers?"

"Primarily to reduce the risk of war. Beginning with the first annexations of their neighbors by

Massachusetts and Pennsylvania in the 18th century, mistrust between these nations was the norm in the Britannic region. Once tensions between these countries were reduced, the reformers turned their focus on improving the region's economy. Those issues are still being hashed out today."

"What would you say are the economic issues that could undo the agreement of this congress?"

"Trade barriers and tariffs, primarily. Also, the adoption of a regional currency. As it stands now, each nation issues its own money. That will change if—"

Wuhao touched his earpiece, then interrupted her. "I'm sorry professor. I'm told the speaker of the congress will be addressing the delegates."

The split screen with the professor disappeared.

A wide shot of the convention floor tracked the approach toward the podium of a tall man in a business suit. The crowd quieted. Arriving at the podium's bank of microphones, the speaker said, "I'm told all the delegations have made their decisions. We'll now take a roll call vote on the ratification of the American Union agreement," he said solemnly.

Turning toward the table at the far right, the speaker said, "Georgia?"

"Aye," the head delegate said into the microphone at his table.

Moving his gaze to the next table, the speaker said, "North Carolina?"

"Aye," came the reply.

"Massachusetts?"

"Aye."

"Pennsylvania?"

"Aye."

"South Carolina?"

"Aye."

"Virginia?"

The head delegate turned toward her colleagues, scanning their faces. The entire hall grew still.

Leaning toward the microphone, she said, "Aye."

In a deafening roar, the crowd rose to their feet.

After a time, the speaker raised his palms, calming the audience. "We have one final decision to announce before we conclude," he said. "The permanent location for future meetings of the American Union will be built at an unincorporated site near Chesapeake Bay. This new district will be named Jefferson."

The audience roared its approval again.

The American Union was taking its first steps.

***

After her interview, Dorothy watched the rest of the CCTV broadcast, wiping tears from her cheeks. Could her parents have imagined this day?

Dorothy had been fourteen before Olivia and Brody revealed the truth about their lives. Once she learned their story, she understood why they'd lied.

Her parents left Francia as fugitives wanted by the security agencies of Virginia, Pennsylvania, Francia and the USSR. Their escape was a tribute to their savvy.

After leaving Francia, Olivia and Brody traveled through a number of countries, creating new identities in each. They became Russian dolls, hiding one identity inside another, inside another.

Within the year, the hunt for them cooled. Francia's security agencies were absorbed by the German uprising. As her mother had hoped, the Franks lost interest in a proxy war in the Americas as they suppressed the Teutonic separatist movement.

Olivia and Brody eventually found a haven in Nassau, a backwater where they spoke the language and could blend in. They did more than survive. They learned how to thrive.

The couple bought a small plot of land and grew truck crops as a cover for a business trading digital currencies. Their modest bungalow became the nerve center of an international venture that made a small fortune.

In time, they reconnected with the Patrick Henry Society. Some of the members were in powerful positions. These covert radicals formed the nucleus of the resistance movement that conceived the American Union.

Sadly, her parents never found her namesake, Dorothy Leigh Blake.

Olivia and Brody hadn't taken much when fleeing Paris. But the heirlooms they'd left Dorothy had a place of honor in her bookcase: a worn zippo lighter beside a pair of gold and pink trainers.

Dorothy looked at the mementos and wiped her eyes. Her parents had not lived to see tonight's gathering in New York. But she knew Olivia and Brody would be proud. This moment was theirs.

~=~

TOBACCO REPUBLIC
FACT & FICTION

The fascination in reading an alternative history is imagining how a twist of events in the past might change the world as we know it today. This kind of story, however, only works with a plausible foundation. With that in mind, you may find the historical facts and fiction in *Tobacco Republic* something of a surprise.

NAPOLEON'S INTEREST IN THE AMERICAS

FACT

After winning back the Louisiana territory from Spain in 1800, Napoleon Bonaparte envisioned a French empire in North America with its hub in New Orleans. His cash cow in the hemisphere was the sugar plantations in Haiti. However, the island's slave uprising wiped out that income – and may have changed the course of history. Looking for a new source to fund his wars in Europe, Napoleon chose to sell the Louisiana Territory to the fledgling United States in 1803. Some scholars say Bonaparte believed the territory was ill defined and difficult to defend. Had Napoleon held on to the Louisiana Territory, it's uncertain the United States would have become a coast-to-coast nation.

FICTION

In *Tobacco Republic*, Napoleon does not sell the Louisiana territory to the United States. His victory at the battle of Waterloo changes the course of history.* Napoleon annexes his enemies on the European continent: Austria, Germany and Poland. Then, in a treaty with George III, Napoleon forces England to give up its territories in North America. His ultimate goal is to find the lucrative northwest passage to trade with the orient. With control over a large portion of Europe and most of North America, Napoleon names his new empire Francia. Bonaparte's ambitions are devastating to the Britannic nations. With Francia controlling all the territory west of the Appalachian Mountains, their growth is constrained. Adding to their woes, their economies are dominated by investors from Francia, relegating most Britannic natives to second class status.

*The battle of Waterloo was fought in 1815. The novel alters the historical timeline for dramatic effect.

TOBACCO'S SIGNIFICANCE IN AMERICAN HISTORY

FACT

Long before England's textile mills sparked a demand for cotton during the industrial revolution, tobacco was the primary cash crop of colonial America. Tobacco was not only a major export commodity, it was even used as a form of currency in Virginia, Maryland and North Carolina. To meet the high demand for tobacco exports, colonial growers came to rely on indentured servants and later enslaved workers. The plantation economy based on unpaid labor that emerged in the tobacco growing regions of the southern colonies would stoke an economic and political conflict with the mercantile colonies of the north, culminating in the U.S. Civil War.

FICTION

In *Tobacco Republic,* control of the lucrative tobacco fields ignites an ongoing source of conflict between the nations of Pennsylvania and Virginia. The cotton gin is never invented in the novel, preventing the shift from tobacco to cotton plantations that actually occurred in the U.S. South.

THE LEE RESOLUTION

FACT

The Lee Resolution was proposed by Richard Henry Lee of Virginia and adopted by the Continental Congress on July 2, 1776. Unlike Jefferson's Declaration of Independence that sought to justify the ideological values of the colonists' cause for an international audience, the Lee Resolution was a brief procedural document initiating the process of independence within the Continental Congress. Here is the full text of the Lee Resolution:

> *Resolved, That these United Colonies are, and of right ought to be, free and independent States, that they are absolved from all allegiance to the British Crown, and that all political connection between them and the State of Great Britain is, and ought to be, totally dissolved.*
>
> *That it is expedient forthwith to take the most effectual measures for forming foreign Alliances.*
>
> *That a plan of confederation be prepared and transmitted to the respective Colonies for their consideration and approbation.*

FICTION

In Tobacco Republic, Thomas Jefferson's Declaration of Independence is rejected in favor of the Lee Resolution.

EUROPEAN IMMIGRATION TO NORTH AMERICA

FACT

In the first two centuries following the Declaration of Independence, over 34 million Europeans migrated to the U.S. and became the nation's largest ethnic group.

FICTION

In *Tobacco Republic*, the English-speaking nations of the Britannic region fail to attract a similar wave of European immigrants. The weak economies, political instability and lack of unsettled land in the Britannic nations offers few opportunities for newcomers. The flood of European immigrants in this alternative history arrive in New Francia with its vast, sparsely populated western territory. As a result, people of European descent become a minority in the small, English-speaking nations of the Britannic region. Most of the people in the Britannic region are descendants of former slaves or of indigenous ancestry.

THE INDIGENOUS PEOPLE OF THE THIRTEEN COLONIES

FACT

The arrival of Europeans in the region of the thirteen original colonies drastically changed the human landscape. Within two centuries, the European settlers had almost completely displaced the original inhabitants through disease and warfare. The diminished native populations that remained were forced to relocate west into territories as yet unsettled by Europeans. Historians estimate that by 1776, indigenous people made up just 2-5% of the population of the original thirteen colonies.

FICTION

In *Tobacco Republic*, the Britannic region's Native American nations, although depleted by war and European disease, remain in their ancestral homelands. With France controlling the territory surrounding these English-speaking nations, the European settlers cannot force the indigenous tribes to migrate west (as happened in recorded history). Although a few tribes choose warfare, most choose assimilation, encouraged by Christian missionaries. Without additional waves of migration to the Britannic nations from Europe, descendants of Native Americans become more than a third of the region's diverse ethnic mix.

FACT:

The terms "Jean Crapaud, Johnny Crappeau and Johnny Toad" emerged in England during the Napoleonic Wars, first as an epithet for French sailors, and eventually as a nickname for all French people. The word *crapaud* is French for toad. Some believe the moniker came from the French penchant for eating frogs. But more likely the term evolved from the pre-Christian French coat of arms that featured three toads, later replaced by three irises. In *Tobacco Republic,* "toads" is used to refer to anyone from Francia.

BENJAMIN FRANKLIN'S ANTIPATHY TOWARD GERMAN IMMIGRANTS

FACT:

Benjamin Franklin was a strong advocate for unity among the colonies in 1776. However, Franklin's antipathy to the German newcomers to Pennsylvania is well documented. In 1751 Franklin wrote an essay titled *Observations Concerning the Increase of Mankind*. In that document he addressed German immigration to Pennsylvania. "Why should Pennsylvania, founded by the English, become a Colony of Aliens, who will shortly be so numerous as to Germanize us instead of our Anglifying them, and will never adopt our Language or Customs, any more than they can acquire our Complexion."

FICTION:

In *Tobacco Republic*, Franklin voices his displeasure with German immigration to Pennsylvania as a reason to reject Jefferson's cause for unity among the colonies. As historical facts show, this artistic license is not completely unfounded.

THOMAS JEFFERSON'S PARADOX OF IDEALS

FACT:

In the Declaration of Independence, Thomas Jefferson assailed the injustices of British taxation, concluding that all men were endowed by their creator with unalienable rights to life, liberty, and the pursuit of happiness. At the time he wrote those words, Jefferson held nearly 100 human beings in bondage. The contradictions did not end there. Most historians agree that Jefferson's intimate relationship with Sally Hemings, an enslaved servant in his household, produced six children. Jefferson never acknowledged their paternity but did free his offspring. No other enslaved people in his household were freed. In his own way, Jefferson remained a man of principle. Instead of arriving at his inauguration in a carriage accompanied by a military detail, Thomas Jefferson chose to walk from his hotel to his swearing-in ceremony with a few friends. Jefferson was the first president inaugurated in the new U.S. capital of Washington, D.C. in 1801.

FICTION:

Tobacco Republic accurately depicts Jefferson's walk to his inauguration. The novel speculates on details of Jefferson's relationship with Sally Hemings and her descendants.

BENJAMIN FRANKLIN OWNED SLAVES

FACT:

Franklin's relationship with slavery was complicated. In his earlier years he owned as many as seven enslaved people and profited from the institution by selling runaway slave ads in his publications. Later in life, he changed his stance and became something of an abolitionist. His reasons for opposing slavery were not altogether altruistic. "Why increase the Sons of Africa, by Planting them in America, where we have so fair an Opportunity, by excluding all Blacks and Tawneys, of increasing the lovely White and Red?" In that same document, Franklin also stated: "The Whites who have Slaves, not labouring, are enfeebled, and therefore not so generally prolific." The document also included a less than generous assumption: "almost every Slave being by Nature a Thief."

FICTION:

The characters of Peter and Jemima in *Tobacco Republic* are portrayals of real-life enslaved servants in Franklin's household. In Franklin's will, both were freed upon his death.

ROBERT E. LEE FREED HIS SLAVES

FACT

While Robert E. Lee claimed slavery was "a moral and political evil," he never willingly freed any of the nearly 200 enslaved people he inherited. He was forced to grant their freedom by his father-in-law's will. The historical Lee never proposed freeing slaves willing to fight for the South. However, that was suggested by an Irish-born Confederate general named Patrick Cleburne. The leadership of the confederacy rejected Cleburne's idea. (The portrayal of Robert E. Lee as an educator in *Tobacco Republic* is historically accurate. Following his stint as General-In-Chief of the confederate army, Lee retired to become president of Washington University in 1865. The school was later renamed Washington and Lee University.)

FICTION

In *Tobacco Republic*, Robert E. Lee frees some of his slaves to fight in Virginia's war against Pennsylvania. That decision ignites a chain of events that ends with a massive northern migration of enslaved people of African descent fleeing the tobacco-growing plantations in Virginia, North and South Carolina, and Georgia. The arrival of these former slaves in Pennsylvania, New York and Massachusetts significantly alters the ethnic composition of these nations. With Native Americans already a large percentage of the population, people of European descent become a minority in all the Britannic nations.

PAULINE SAVARI, AN EARLY FEMINIST

FACT & FICTION:

Born in France in 1859, Pauline Savari was a journalist, novelist, union organizer, a promoter of women's arts and crafts, and an advocate for improved maternal conditions. In *Tobacco Republic*, Pauline is fictionally portrayed as the author of a book about the Britannic region. She never wrote such a book and was not the niece of a publisher.

FACT

The practice of the freshman Rat Line and the motto "never, never die" are part of the long-held traditions at the Virginia Military Academy. Both were incorporated into Olivia Braxton's character in *Tobacco Republic*.

THE SOVIET UNION

FACT

The Soviet Union's growth into a world power paralleled that of the United States. Both nations rose to global dominance in the twentieth century. Born of an upheaval that began in 1913, the USSR became one of the most powerful nations on earth until its collapse in 1991. The peak of Soviet power began in the late 1940s and sparked a Cold War with the United States. While vying for international supremacy, the USA and USSR were constrained from direct conflict by the nuclear weapons each possessed. Instead they battled through subterfuge and surrogates. Smaller countries were sometimes armed and supported by the superpowers. These proxy wars took place in Korea, Vietnam, Nicaragua and Angola, to name a few.

FICTION

In *Tobacco Republic*, Francia and the USSR are superpowers that use the Britannic region in their Cold War games. The novel portrays a Soviet Union that avoids a 20th century implosion and survives into the 21st century by curbing military spending and loosening its state-controlled economy.

Have any comments or questions?
Please visit our blog at: Author-R-A-Moss.com

AUTHOR R. A. MOSS

R. A. Moss earned his keep as a writer long before penning KING ROBIN and TOBACCO REPUBLIC. Under his birth name, he authored four novels in other genres that earned accolades from Library Journal, Publishers Weekly, and USA Today.

Visit his website at: Author-R-A-Moss.com

Enjoyed TOBACCO REPUBLIC?
Please consider leaving an honest review online at your favorite merchant.

OTHER WORK BY R. A. MOSS

WHAT IF... Robin Hood became king?
Spanning a half-century in the life and times of Robin
Hood, this action packed and erotic Medieval thriller
vividly explores the seductive undertow of power as it
transforms a legendary hero into a ruthless tyrant.

Learn more at: king-robin-novel.com